영원히
불
타오르는
이되어

이 작은 시집을
유관순 열사와 조국의 애국 선열들께
기도드리는 마음으로 바친다.

영원히 불 타오르는 별이 되어

장철우 시 | 김리자 영역

선우미디어 sunwoomedia

책을 내면서

초등학교 때 아버지가 나에게 첫번 주신 책이 《유관순 전》(전영택 지음)이었다. 그때 어린 내마음에 열사의 애국혼이 각인되었다고 할까.

한국동란을 겪으며 피난생활과 중고등학교를 졸업하고 곧바로 아버지의 뜻에 따라 신학을 공부하고 군복무를 마쳤다. 몇 년 후 미국 유학생활과 교회 개척, 50여 년을 목회에 전념했다.

은퇴 후 한국을 방문하여 서점에 들러 유관순 열사에 대한 책을 찾았으나 몇 개의 서점을 뒤진 후에야 겨우 찾을 수 있었다. 실망한 나머지 내가 열사에 대한 책을 쓰리라 뜻을 세운 지 10년이 훨씬 넘었다. 지금은 많은 유관순 전기가 나왔다. 기쁜 일이다.

나는 마음을 바꾸어 유관순에 대한 신앙심과 애국혼을 찾아 시로 표현하여 전달하기로 하였다. 5년 동안 열사를 마음에 품고 영적 대화의 길을 찾았다. 묵상과 기도를 통해 열사가 가진 신앙심과 애국의 열정을 자신의 경험으로 느끼며 표현하려고 애썼다. 쉽지 않았다.

그러나 새로운 배움과 보람을 얻게 된 것이 있었다. 그것은 새로운 민족의식과 배달겨레의 정체성이다. 유관순 열사가 하느님 주신 사명

속에서 애국혼을 불태우며 그 생명까지 바치는 고귀한 뜻은 만년의 역사를 타고 내려온 조상들이 물려준 유산의 결과임을 알았다.

남강의 논개, 낙화암의 백제 궁녀들, 행주치마의 유래를 남겨준 행주산성의 여인들, 심청의 효성 등. 이 뿐이랴, 안시성의 양만춘, 을지문덕, 관창, 계백장군, 정몽주의 충정, 이순신의 백의종군, 안중근 윤봉길 등 이들의 애국충정의 넋 또한 맥을 같이한다. 여기서 대한 조국의 정체성을 찾았다. 만년을 이어오며 다져진 것이요 민족의 생존을 지켜준 위대한 얼이다. 하나님이 주신 것이기에 동해물이 마르고 백두산이 닳도록 우리의 대한을 지켜주시었다.

조국은 남북으로 갈려 있다. 정치 이념도 벽을 쌓았다. 지방 색, 빈부 차이에서 오는 반목 등 사분오열 되어 있다. 통합을 말하고 타협을 애쓴다. 자기 정체성을 잃은 민족은 통합이 불가능하다.

이스라엘은 종교심에서, 선민의식 속에서 자기 정체성을 확립하였다. 늦지 않았다. 통일을 원하는가 통합을 원하는가 대화의 합일을 원하는가, 이제 그동안 잊어버렸든 잃어버렸던 민족의 정체성을 찾아야 한다. 기억해야 한다.

나는 유관순 열사를 그리며 그의 생애와 신앙, 애국심에서 이 고귀한 뜻을 깨달았다. 이 시집을 집필하여 감히 내놓는 이유가 여기 있다.

2022년 5월
뉴욕에서 장철우

On Writing the Book

The first book that my father gave me in elementary school was a biography of Kwan Soon Yu by Young Taek Jeun. The spirit of the patriotic martyr must have been imprinted in my young heart at that time. Living as a refugee amidst the turmoil of the Korean war, I finished high school and studied pastoral theology at a seminary as my father wished. I finished my military obligation in the Korean army, too. A few years later I came to the United States of America to study theology. I devoted 50 years of my life on church planting and pastoral ministry. After my retirement, I went back to South Korea. While I was in Seoul, I visited a few book stores to look for biographies of Kwan Soon Yu. To my disappointment, I did not find that many books on her life. I decided to write her biography myself. That was more than 10 years ago. Since then, many books on her life have been published. I am happy about that.

Instead of biography, I decided to write poems on her faith and patriotic spirit. I explored a way to open spiritual dialogues with her for five years. I tried to experience her faith and patriotic spirit in my own heart through meditations and prayers, and wanted to express them in poetry.

It was not easy. Yet it was worthwhile and new learning experience for me.

I was able to get new identity of national consciousness as a Korean. I think God's mission for patriot Kwan Soon Yu that consumed her patriotic soul and sacrificed her life was possible because of the inheritance from our ancestors of ten thousands of years. The patriotic spirits of Non Gae of Nam River, court ladies of Baekjae Kingdom at Nakhwaahm, women of Haengjusan Fortress who left tradition of apron, Shimcheong of filial piety, Yang Manchun of Ansi City, General Eulji Mundeok of Koguryeo Kingdom, Gwanchang of Shilla, General Gyebaek, Chung Mong Ju, white army of Admiral Yi Sun-shin, An Jung-geun and Yoon Bong-gil, run in the blood stream of Korean people. I found my Korean identity in them. This great spirit has been established and molded over thousands and thousands of years and kept our national identity alive. Since it is a gift from God, it will guard our nation until the East Sea dries up and Beakdu Mountain wears off. Now the South and North are divided. Our political ideology is different, too.

Regionalism, and the gap between the rich and poor have divided our nation. We try unification. Unification becomes impossible when the nation loses its identity. Israel was able to establish its national identity firmly with commoner's consciousness because of their religious beliefs. It is not too late. Most important thing is recovering our forgotten national identity whether we want unification or not. We have to remember. Honoring patriot Kwan Soon Yu, I realized the lofty meaning of her life, faith and patriotism.

That is why I wrote this book of poems.

May, 2022 In New York

목차

[첫 번째 묶음]
나라사랑 Love of Country

장철우 시인의 유관순을 기리는 시를 읽고서

최병현 (시인)

불과 100년 전만 해도 독립이나 애국은 사랑만큼이나 열렬한 시적 감정이었다. 시대가 빠르게 급변하다보니 시의 주제로서 독립이나 애국은 어느덧 자유나 평등에게 자리를 내주고, 나라 사랑은 남녀의 사랑에게 자리를 빼앗긴 채 설 자리를 잃고 말았다. 어쩌다 누군가 불쑥 나라 사랑을 노래하면 의아한 눈으로 바라보게 되고, 개인주의적인 연정에 익숙해진 세대는 조율이 안 된 악기 연주에 반응하듯 음악이기에 앞서 시대와의 불협화음을 느끼게 된다.

장철우 시인의 유관순에 대한 연모의 시 역시 예외는 아니다. 사람들의 기억에서 사라져 삼일절에나 생각나는 이름을 소월의 '초혼'처럼 간절히 소리쳐 부르니, 한용운의 '님'이 무색하리만큼 자기는 유관순을 보내지 않았다고 강변하니, 세월의 벽에 막힌 시적 감흥이 달리는 지하철에서 간혹 접속 장애를 일으키는 휴대전화 소리처럼 들리기도 하는 것이다. 그리 생각하면 유관순의 시는 100년 전에 태어났더라면 좋았을 것이다. 그 시절로 돌아갈 수만 있다면, 시인의 주장처럼 유관순이 한국의 잔다크라 해도 하등 이의를 제기할 사람도 없고, 팔순의 노인이 비극적인 삶을 살다간 소녀를 "누나"라 불러도 "좋아요"를 누를 것이다. 그렇다면 이제 애국시의 시대는 영원히 끝난 것인가? 유관순이란 이름과 연시에 등장하는 주인공 이름은 더 이상 각운이 맞지 않는 것일까?

세월이 흐르고 역사가 바뀌어 우리의 감수성에 문제가 생겼다면, 앞으로도 시대는 바뀌고 감수성 또한 변할 것이기에, 유관순을 기억하고자 하는 애국시 또한 다시 부활하지 않을까? 나라가 있는 한 나라 사랑이 이상할 것이 없는데, 나라 사랑과 유관순에 대한 사랑이 동의어처럼 느껴지는 세상이 오지 않으리라고 어찌 단언할 수 있겠는가?

9·11의 도시에 사는 사람들이 떠난 자들의 이름을 돌에 새겼듯이, 장철우 시인의 선창으로 유관순의 이름을 부르는 것이 유행할지 어찌 알겠는가? 그렇다면 유관순을 노래한 시인은 또 다른 백년을 바라본 것이 아닌가.

장 시인의 유관순 시는 말의 아름다움보다는 뜻의 아름다움이 돋보인다. 감정을 가공해 꾸민 허망한 말보다는 진심의 울림이 있는 뜻의 시가 절실할 때, 한번쯤 무대에 출연해야 하는 시가 바로 장철우 시인이 눈물의 소금에 절여 굴비처럼 엮어 내놓은 유관순을 기리는 시이다. 그의 시에는 "나를 제물로 삼으소서"라고 기도하는 절규의 메아리가 에밀레 종소리처럼 절절하다. 맹인처럼 앞을 못 보는 나라, 그의 눈을 뜨게 하기 위해 심청이가 된 유관순의 일편단심이 고귀하게 느껴진다.

꽃다발을 받을 때 우리는 꽃보다 마음을 받게 된다. 시도 마찬가지. 꽃은 시들고 향기는 사라져도 넋으로 변한 마음은 말없이 사계절을 지키는 정원처럼 원래의 자리에 머물기 때문이다.

　　뉴욕 방문 시, 장철우 목사께서 문득 시를 보여 주시기에 사양하면서 書하다.

After Reading Paul Chang's Poems Honoring Kwan Soon Yu

Even one hundred years ago, independence and patriotism were as popular themes of poetry as love. Time has been changing rapidly. Now independence and patriotism have been replaced by freedom and equality as poetry themes.

Patriotism has lost its place and been replaced by love between a man and woman. If anybody sings about patriotism once in a while, he/she has been looked upon as archaic. The generation that became accustomed to individualistic love senses it is out of sync with the time and responds as if they are putting up with disharmonious music just because it is music. Paul Chang's poems honoring Kwan Soon Yu are no exceptions. He is desperately calling a name that disappeared from people's memory, a name that comes up only at March 1st Independence Day as if it were the name in 'First Soul' by So—wol Kim. His insistence not to let go of Kwan Soon Yu makes Nim in The Silence of Nim by Yong Woon Han look pale in comparison. His poetic inspiration that's walled up by time was like listening to cell phone in subway train with intermittent internet connection. Poems on Kwan Soon Yu would have been received with much more enthusiasm if they were published one hundred years ago.

If we can go back to that time, nobody would object to the idea that Kwan Soon Yu was indeed Joan of Arc of Korea. Yet, is the time of patriotic poetry over for good? If we have problems in our sensitivity because time and history bring new chapters, our perceptions will keep evolving in the future. There may be a revival for patriotic poetry to remember Kwan Soon Yu in the future. As long as there is a country, there is bound to be love for the country. Who knows? In the future, there may come a time when the name, Kwan Soon Yu, and love of country may be used synonymously. As people who lived in the cities attacked by terrorists on September 11 etched the names of victims on monuments, calling the name, Kwan Soon Yu, may catch on with poet Paul Chang's leadership. Then, the poet who honors Kwan Soon Yu must have been looking ahead into one hundred years. These poems on the patriot by Paul Chang stand out because of the beauty of meaning rather than beauty of words. His poems reverberate with truth instead of futile words of falsified emotions. They deserve a place on the stage. His poems honoring Kwan Soon Yu are like dried corvinas on straw strings soaked with his tears and salt. His poems are so full of howling echoes of prayers like 'let me be the sacrificial offering' that they touch our hearts deeply like the sound of Emile bell. Single—hearted devotion on Kwan Soon Yu who became Shim—Cheung to open the eyes of the nation that could not see the future sounds honorable. When we receive bouquet, we receive heart. Poems are similar. Flowers may dry up and their scents may go away, but our thankful hearts remember them like a garden that blooms throughout four seasons.

During my visit to New York, Reverend Paul Chang showed me his poems. I read them humbly.

January 28, 2022

유관순 누나를 생각합니다

삼월 하늘 가만히 우러러보며
유관순 누나를 생각합니다.
옥중에 갇혔어도 만세 부르다
푸른 하늘 그리며 숨이 졌대요

삼월 하늘 가만히 우러러보며
유관순 누나를 불러 봅니다.
지금도 그 목소리 들릴 듯하여
푸른 하늘 우러러 불러봅니다.

– 강소천 작사, 나운영 작곡

삼월이 되면 파도가 밀려오듯 삼일절과 더불어 유관순 열사를 그리
게 됩니다.

유관순은 삼일 혁명의 꽃입니다. 처음으로 유관순의 전기를 쓴 전영

택 목사는 프랑스혁명의 꽃이 잔 다르크라면 대한민국 삼일 혁명의 꽃은 유관순 열사다."라고 했습니다.

잔 다르크가 영국군에 붙잡혀 화형을 당하면서도 애국충정의 뜻을 굽히지 않았습니다. 유관순은 어떤 고문을 당하였는가, 감옥에서 순국하기 전 남겨놓은 애국충정의 고백을 보면 알 수 있습니다. "내 손톱이 빠져나가고 내 귀와 코가 잘리고 내 다리가 부러져도 그 고통은 이길 수 있사오나 나라를 잃은 고통만은 견딜 수 없습니다. 나라에 바칠 목숨이 아직 하나밖에 없는 것이 이 소녀의 유일한 슬픔입니다." 유관순이 마지막 토해낸 절규의 고백이었습니다. 형무소 기록에 열사의 사인은 '방광과 자궁 파열'이라고 적혀 있습니다.

이것이 유관순의 마지막까지 보여준 애국충정의 모습입니다.

유관순 열사가 남겨준 애국혼과 얼은 지금도 살아있어 조국 대한의 역사를 자손만대까지 길이길이 지켜 주리라 확신합니다.

몇 년 전 유관순 열사의 고향과, 그가 다녔던 공주의 영명, 서울의 이화학교를 둘러보고 순국한 서대문형무소를 답사하였습니다. 애국의 발자취를 따르는 순례의 여정이었습니다.

여권 기일이 다 되어 조국을 떠나기 마지막 밤에 꿈을 꾸었습니다. 그토록 보고 싶었던 그분의 영상이 그리움을 채워주듯 나타난 것입니다. 저는 그 생생했던 꿈의 장면을 적어 놓았습니다. 특히 열사가 우리에게 마지막 주고 싶은 말씀은 무엇이었을까. 고인은 말이 없었습니다. 그러나 저는 그 꿈속에서 그분의 마지막 말씀을 듣는 듯 하였습니다.
　꿈의 영상을 적겠습니다.

"영원히 불타오르는 별이 되어."

　하늘의 별빛도 찬란히 빛을 그으며 오다가 오다가 지쳐 사그라지는데 당신의 빛은 다가오면 올수록 더 크고 아름답게 가슴으로 저며 들어오고 있습니다.
　별빛은 한 빛인데 당신의 빛은 색색의 빛깔을 다 가지고 빛으로 타오르니 무슨 빛이라 말할 수 없군요. 하늘의 진주 빛이 그러합니까, 하늘의 보석 빛이 그러합니까? 보면 볼수록 커지는 별, 눈부시도록 진하게 다가오는 빛, 조국 삼천리 강토에 비춰어 민족의 가슴에 영원히 비취는 그 빛, 유관순 순국열사의 별빛이라 그러합니까?

　저는 당신의 빛을 찾아 순례의 여정을 마치고 돌아오는 날 밤 밤새껏 꿈을 꾸었습니다.

　바로 유관순이 다닌 이화학교의 난간이 보였습니다.
　머리를 땋고 흰 저고리에 검정 치마의 교복을 입은 학생들이 교실밖

난간 위에 나란히 서 있었습니다. 그런데 한 가운데 학생들 틈 사이에 유난히 빛나는 별빛이 있었습니다. 일곱색의 영롱한 빛은 제 눈이 부시도록 빛났습니다. 잠시 후 그 빛이 어디론가 향할 때 제 혼이 빛 속에 빨려들듯 빛을 따라갔습니다. 그 빛은 별이 되어 이화의 교정을 천천히 한 바퀴 돌더니 저를 이끌고 남쪽으로 내려갑니다. 어느 사이 산을 넘더니 며칠 전 제가 찾아보았던 병천 지령리에 있는 유관순 집에 머물렀습니다. 이리저리 방들과 대청마루와 뜰을 둘러보고는 우물가 냇가로 내려갑니다. 그리고 마을로 향하더니 한참이나 마을 위를 맴돌았습니다. 그리고 만세 시위를 벌인 병천시장으로 갔습니다. 유관순의 아버지, 어머니가 일본 순사의 총칼을 맞고 순국하신 그 자리에서 한참이나 움직이지 않았습니다. 별도 울고 있는 것일까. 이윽고 별은 움직이더니 병촌시장을 내려다보듯 우뚝 솟은 매봉산으로 올라갑니다. 산기슭으로 저를 이끈 별은 산정상을 오르며 영롱한 일곱색을 보이며 진하게 타오르듯 그 빛을 찬란히 비추었습니다. 마침내 정상에 올랐을 때 별빛이 멈추더니 봉홧불이 되어 타올랐습니다. 눈부시도록 찬란했던 별빛이 봉홧불로 변하면서 온 천지를 환하게 밝히는 것입니다. 하늘도 대지도 환하게 대낮처럼 밝혔습니다. 마치 영원히 영원히 꺼지지 않을 것처럼 밝혔습니다.

새벽에 눈을 떴습니다. 너무도 생생한 꿈이었습니다. 꿈에 보았던 찬란한 별빛과 매봉산에서 온 세상을 환히 밝힌 봉홧불은 내 가슴, 아니 내 몸 전체에서 사라지지 않았습니다.

그토록 그리워하던 유관순 열사를 내 영혼이 만날 수 있었다는 것이 너무 기뻤습니다. 너무 감사하였습니다. 새벽에 무릎 꿇고 두 손 모아 감사의 기도를 드렸습니다. 영원히 내 영혼 속에 불타오르게 하소서.

잠시 후 몇 가지 의문이 떠올랐습니다.

유관순 열사가 붙잡혀간 헌병구치소, 공주법원, 서대문형무소, 잔인하게 고문당한 지하 고문실 등은 왜 안내하지 않았을까.

만 16세 나이에 나라에 대한 사랑과 그리고 하나님의 뜻과 사명을 간직하였던 신앙심은 나라의 원수요 자기 부모를 죽인 원수, 자신을 고문하여 방광과 자궁이 터져 죽임을 당한 일본에 대하여 기억조차 하기 싫었던 것일까.

유관순 열사의 숭고한 심령 속에는 맑은 진실, 사랑, 그리고 나라 사랑의 사명만이 가득했기에 자기가 당한 고통과 분노, 증오와 원수가 깨끗한 마음에 자리할 수가 없었습니다. 마치 하늘나라에는 거짓과 분노, 증오, 원수가 없듯이 하늘나라에서 내려와 저에게 보인 별빛은 그토록 진실과 사랑이 넘쳤기에 열사가 당했던 고통과 증오의 몸부림친 장소와 시간은 다 사라졌던 것입니다. 마치 별빛이 타오르는 봉화가 되어 세상의 악한 것들은 모두 태워버렸습니다. 어둠을 불사르고 사랑과 의로운 광명의 세계로 변화시켰던 것입니다.

이것이 제 의문의 답이었습니다.

나는 유관순 열사의 전기를 읽을 때마다 나도 모르게 주먹을 쥐었고 터질 듯 뛰는 심장을 누르며 눈시울이 뜨거워지곤 하였습니다. 그러나 열사의 꿈을 꾸고 난 후 열사의 갸륵한 애국혼, 순국에까지 이른 그의 신앙심만을 가슴에 담기로 하였습니다.

더욱이 열사의 뒷동산인 매봉산에 오를 때 확실해졌습니다.

유관순의 후예인 이화의 학생들이 때묻지 않은 손으로 언니가 남겨준 애국혼과 신앙심을 따라 돌비석에 새겨놓은 시들이 줄을 이어 세워져 있었습니다.

푸른 하늘처럼 맑았고 산봉우리처럼 줄기찼습니다.

끝없는 하늘에 이르기까지 비석의 시들이 이어졌습니다.

영원토록 영원토록 열사의 후예들은 그 시들을 이어갈 것입니다.

꺼지지 않는 별빛, 타오르는 봉화의 불이 되어 민족의 가슴에 그리고 한반도 대한민국에 영원히 비취이리라.

나도 모르게 100여 년 전 유관순으로 돌아가 그가 품었던 시상을 떠올리며 순수한 시로 남기고 싶었습니다.

2022년 5월
장철우

Thinking of Kwon Soon Yu

Looking up into the March sky in silence,

I am thinking of Kwan Soon Yu.

Even in the prison,

She shouted 'Long Live Korea' for her nation.

She drew her last breath, longing to see the blue sky.

Looking up into the March sky in silence,

I am thinking of Kwan Soon Yu.

As if I could hear her voice now,

I am looking up at the blue sky.

Lyrics by So Cheun Kang, Music composed by Un Young Nah

Thoughts of Kwan Soon Yu comes to me like ocean waves on March Independence Day. She is the flower of March Revolution. Pastor Young Taek Chun who wrote her first biography compared her to Joan of Arc, the flower of French revolution. Joan of Arc never gave up her patriotism even when she was captured by English soldiers and put on a burning stake. The confession of Kwan Soon Yu's patriotism during her imprisonment tells us what kind of tortures she endured. "I can bear the pain of losing my fingers, my ears, my nose, and my legs. But I cannot bear the pain of losing my own country. I am sorry I have only one life to give for my country." These words were her last confession. According to the prison record, the cause of her death was rupture of bladder and uterus. Her spirit of patriotism is still alive and will live forever as an exemplary model for generations to come.

A few years ago, I visited Kwan Soon Yu's home town, her alma mater, Young Myung School, Ewha School, and West Gate Prison where she finally passed away. It was a patriotic pilgrimage for me. I had a dream on that trip. She appeared in my dream one night as if she wanted to acknowledge my admiration for her and my wish to meet her. I wrote about that dream. She was silent in that dream. I wondered what last message the patriotic martyr wanted to give us. I felt I heard that message in that dream. I am going to write about it.

"Becoming a Star That Glows Forever"

Even the glow of numerous stars in the sky becomes tired, dimming on their travel, but your light becomes brighter as time passes.

The light of stars is one color, but your glow has many colors that I cannot even describe. Is it the color of pearl in the sky? Or is it the color of jewel in the sky? The longer I look up at your glow, the more it grows larger and brighter. Is it so bright because it is the patriotic light that glows forever in the hearts of Korean people?

I had a dream one night on my pilgrimage to seek your light. In my dream, I saw a railing at your alma mater, Ewha Hakdang. I saw a line of students standing at the railing, dressed in black and white school uniform and with their hair braided. I noticed one unusually bright light among those students. The light of seven colors almost blinded me. As the light moved, I followed it in trance. The light became a star. It slowly walked around Ewha campus and led me to the south. The star led me over mountains and valleys. Soon I found myself at Kwan Soon Yu's house at Chi Ryung Ri in Byung Chun. I looked around her house; living room and garden. Then I went to the well. I went to the village and roamed around for a long time. Then I went to Byung Chun Market where the Long Live Korea Demonstration was held. I stayed there motionless. That was the place where Kwan Soon Yu's parents were martyred by Japanese soldiers. Is the star crying? Soon the star started to move and went up to the Mae Bong Mountain that looked over the Byung Chun Market. The star drew me near the mountain. It shined with seven bright colors. It climbed to the top of the mountain and became beacon that shone all over the world. The whole world was lit up by that star. The light seemed to shine to eternity. I opened my eyes next morning. My dream felt very real. The bright light, the beacon at the top of the mountain I saw in dream stayed in my heart and soul. I was very happy that my soul finally encountered Kwan Soon Yu, the Korean patriotic martyr. I knelt and said a prayer of gratitude. Let her love of Korea stay in my soul forever!

Later, few questions came to me.

Why didn't the star guide me to the Japanese military police station where she stayed, Gongju Court, and West Gate Prison where she was tortured?

Was it because I did not want to remember Japanese atrocities committed to the 16 years old girl who loved her country and had faith to carry out her mission according to God's will? There's no room for pain, anger, and animosity in the holy soul of Kwan Soon Yu except truth, love and patriotism. As there are no anger, hatred, enemy and lies in the heaven, the light that came down from heaven to lead me was so full of love and truth that it made the place and time of pain and torture she suffered disappear.

Whenever I read biography of Kwan Soon Yu, I used to clench my hands, and felt my heart racing and tears in my eyes. After the dream during my pilgrimage, I decided to cherish only her admirable patriotic soul and her faith that led to martyrdom. That determination became more solid when I was at the Mae Bong Mountain near her hometown. There were many stone monuments that had numerous writings on her patriotic spirit and Christian faith by Ewha alumnae. The writings were as clear as blue sky and steadfast as mountain top. There were endless writings of tribute. Generation after generation the tributes will continue to be written.

She will be the inextinguishable light of star and the beacon of everlasting flame in the deep souls of Koreans. I traveled back to the time when Kwan Soon Yu lived and wanted to express my thoughts in poems as tributes to her life.

첫 번째 묶음

나라 사랑
Love of Country

사진 설명 : 개교 100주년을 맞은 영명중·고등학교는 학교 교내에 유관순 열사 기념
관과 동상을 세웠다.
유관순은 사부인 선교사(사에리시)의 도움으로 사부인이 세운 공주 영명(여자) 학교
에 입학하여(1914~1915년) 보통과를 수료케 되었으며 사부인의 도움으로 이화학당
으로 편입하였다. (1916~1919년)

유관순의 노래

내가 처음 한글을 배웠을 때
하나님 사랑, 나라 사랑을 읽었습니다

내가 처음 노래를 배웠을 때
예수 사랑, 애국가를 불렀습니다

내가 처음 꿈을 꾸었을 때
태극기 손에 들고 내 나라 독립을 외치는
대한 독립 만세의 꿈이었습니다

대한 독립 그것을 위해
놀이터에서도, 예배당에서도, 학교에서도, 빨래터 위에서도
열심히 하였습니다

공주 영명, 서울 이화 학교에서 만난 선생님들은
애국의 씨알을 키워 주었습니다

고향의 교회, 정동의 교회 목사님들은 하나님 나라
대한 조국의 환상을 보여 주었습니다

마침내 기도하는 소녀가 되었습니다
간절한 기도 응답의 실현을 보았습니다
그것은 나의 사명, 하나님이 주신 사명이 되었습니다

교정에서, 덕수궁 담을 돌면서, 병천 장터에서 대한 독립 만세를 외쳤습니다

나의 사명이기 때문입니다

일본 순사, 헌병의 총칼에 부모를 잃고
형무소 모진 고문에 내 생명이 다할 때
어릴 때 꿈꾸었던 나라 사랑, 대한 독립이 무엇인지
알게 되었습니다

내가 가진 사명은 지금도 살아있습니다.

대한 나라의 빛과 바람 그리고 물

대한 조국의 흙 속에 당신의 흘린 피가 배었나요
조국을 비추는 태양 빛에 당신의 뜨거운 애국혼이 배었나요
아침이슬, 흐르는 강물 위에 겨레 사랑의 얼이 흐르고 있나요?
조선반도 해맑은 바람에 당신의 청렴한 애국정신이 배었나요

뜨거운 태양 볕에서 숨이 차고
땀방울 짜내며 몸이 갈증이 날 때
당신의 얼을 코로, 입으로 마시나이다

당신의 혼이 묻힌 대지 위에서
생명으로 이끄는 태양 빛을 따라
당신의 애국 씨알이 영글어 갑니다

대한 독립 만세
나도 목소리 다해 외칠 수 있습니다
당신이 남긴 대지에 우뚝 서서

저 태양을 향해
숨을 다해 토해내며
해맑은 물 마셔가며
영구히 영구히
대한 독립 만세 부르리이다.

나의 노래

나의 노래는 대한 독립의 노래, 만세의 노래

나의 노래는 나라 사랑의 노래
삼천리 화려강산을 노래하네

나의 노래는 겨레를 사랑하는 노래
천하보다 귀한 생명을 찬양하는 노래

드높은 하늘에 울려 퍼지네
온 땅에 두루 퍼지네

나의 목소리가 노래하네
나의 손과 발이 노래하네
세포 구석구석에서
뼈마디 마디 속에서 노래하네

산에서 들에서도 노래하리
바다에서 강가에서도 노래하리
한반도 온 동리 찾아가며 노래하리

끊임없이 노래하리
대한 독립 만세
영구한 노래가 되어
영원히 영원히 노래하리.

그처럼 사랑하셨나요?

동해 물이 마르도록
백두산이 다 닳도록 사랑하셔서
유관순을 보내셨습니까

말씀이 사람이 되었듯이
애국이 화신되어 유관순이 되었습니까

주님의 생애 33년의 절반인데
대한 독립의 화신이 되어
그 몸이 마르고 닳도록
그토록 고통스러운 십자가를 지게 하셨나요?

서대문 감옥 지하 고문실이 골고다였습니까

치욕과 고통의 십자가 그것이 인류구원의 뜻이요 완성이었듯이
모진 고문의 고통 속에서 민족이 영원히 독립할 꿈을 이룩하셨나요?

이제
부활의 아침 새 생명의 영원한 탄생
아침의 나라 한반도에 조선 독립의 영원한 부활을 보았습니다

비로소
마르고 닳도록 사랑하신 하느님께 감사드립니다.

당신은 누구입니까

당신은 누구입니까
대한의 언니, 누나입니까

나라를 가슴에 품고 그토록 사랑하셨기에
산모의 진통을 겪으신 나라의 어머니시지요

당신은 대한의 딸이셨습니까
대한 독립 만세 목숨 다하기까지 외친 소리 진통의 소리보다 더 아픈
민족을 깨우는 소리 소리
그러기에 나라의 어머니시지요

당신은 나라의 친구 그리고 조국의 학도였나요
사지가 찢기도록 피 한 방울 남김없이 나라 위해 바쳤기에
나라 독립의 얼이 되고 혼이 되어
나라 지키는 큰 별처럼 수호신처럼
민족의 가슴에 요동치는 산 맥박 대한 독립의 맥박이었지요

그러기에 당신은 대한 민족의 어머니시지요

그러기에 대한 독립의 어머니시지요

영구히 영구히.

Song of Kwan Soon Yu

When I learned Korean for the first time,
I read love of God, love of country.

When I learned to sing for the first time
I sang love of Jesus and Korean national anthem.

When I had a dream for the first time,
It was a dream of shouting 'Long Live Korea'
Waving a Korean flag.

For independence of Korea,
I did my best at the playground, church, school,
And even when I did laundry.

Teachers I met at Young Myung School in Gongju and Ewha
planted seeds of patriotism.

My home town church and Jung Dong Church instilled in me a
vision for God's kingdom and my country, Korea.

At last, I became a girl who prayed. My prayers were answered,
God gave me a misson.

At the school,
Walking along the wall of Duk Soo Palace,
And at the Byung Chun Market,
I shouted "hurray for independence of Korea".
Because that was my calling.

When my parents were murdered by Japanese military police,
When my life was about to perish because of torture in the
prison,
I realized what love of my country I dreamt as a child was all
about,
I also realized what independence of my home country was all
about.
My mission is still alive.

Light, Wind and Water of My Home Country, Korea

Is the soil of my homeland, Korea, drenched in the blood you
shed?
Is the sunlight that shines over the homeland soaked with your
patriotic soul?
Is the soul of love for our homeland flowing in morning dew
and river?
Is your pure patriotic spirit blowing with the wind all over
Korean peninsula?

When I am out of breath with scorching sun,
When I am thirsty with heavy sweat,
I breathe in and gulp down your spirit.

On the soil where your soul is buried,
Following the sunlight that leads to life,
The seed of your patriotic spirit is maturing.

'Hurray for Independence of Korea'

I can shout with all my strength.

Standing tall on our homeland you left for us,

Toward the sun,

Breathing out with all my strength,

Drinking clear water,

Forever, forever,

I will shout 'Hurray for Independence of Korea'.

My Song

My song is a song of independence of Korea, song of 'Long Live
Korea'

My song is a song of love for my country.
I sing of the beautiful land of Korea, far and wide.

My song is a song of love for my people.
It is a song for life that is more precious than world.

It echoes high into the sky.
It's spreading all over the land.

My voice sings.
My hands and feet are singing.
Every cell in my body is singing.
Every bone in my body is singing.

I will sing on mountains and fields.

I will sing at seas and rivers.

I will sing in every village of Korean peninsula.

I will sing forever. 'Hurray for Independence of Korea'.

It will be a song of eternity.

I will sing to eternity.

Did You Love That Much?

Until the East Sea dries up,
Until the Baek Du Mountain wears down,
You loved us so,
You've sent Kwan Soon Yu to us?

As the Word became life,
Was patriotism personified,
And reincarnated as Kwan Soon Yu?

She lived only half of life time of Our Lord Jesus.
And was personified in Korean independence.
Until her body was totally dried and spent,
She was crucified with unbearable pain.

Was the basement of West Gate Prison Golgotha?

As the cross of humiliation and pain was the only means to complete salvation of the world,
Was the dream of eternal independence accomplished through unbearable pain and torture?

Now,
In the morning of resurrection, birth of eternal and new life,
Eternal resurrection of Korean independence in the Land of Morning Calm was witnessed.

So, I give thanks to God whose love is boundless.

Who Are You?

Who are you?
Are you sister of Korea, older sister?

Because you loved your country so deeply in your heart,
You went through pain of childbirth,
So you are the mother of nation.

Were you a daughter of Korea?
You shouted 'Hurray for Independence of Korea' until your
death,
That exclamation was more painful than labor pain,
It woke up whole nation.
So, you are the mother of Korea.

Were you a friend or a student of our nation?

Because you gave yourself for the homeland until your body
tore apart and your blood dried up,
You became the spirit of Korean independence.
Like a star or patron saint that looks after the nation,
You became the living heartbeat of Korean independence for
entire nation.

So, you are the mother of Korean people,
You are the mother of Korean independence.
Forever and ever.

두 번째 묶음

만 세
Hurray

사진 설명 : 유관순 열사의 고향에 세워진 기념관과 타임캡슐

나의 영원한 님이여

나의 나이 16살
사랑하는 님이 있나이다

언제나 그리운 님
나와 더불어 같이 사는 님

그 이름 한반도 조선 대한 나라
영원히 같이 살아갈 님입니다

영원토록 당신 품 안에서
자유와 평등 누리며
함께 할 님이여
당신의 이름을 목청껏 불러 봅니다

잠을 자도 님을 위해
걸어가도 님을 위해

숨을 쉬어도 님을 위해

대한 조국
당신만을 위하여
나의 절개 지키나이다
당신만을 위하여
내 몸 바치리이다

대한 조국 만세

나의 영원한 님이여
대한 나라 나의 님이여.

대한 독립 만세

대한 독립 만세
온 세상 가득히 메아리칩니다
함성의 소리 장단되어
태극기 하늘에 춤을 춥니다

대한 독립 만세
대지가 출렁이며
산천초목도 손뼉을 칩니다

대한 독립 만세
외치는 소리
뼈마디 마디에 스며들고
저리도록 영혼 속에 새겨집니다

대한 독립 만세
목숨을 바치는 소리

순국의 피가 되어
끝없는 강물처럼
겨레 핏줄 이어 갑니다

대한 독립 만세
산봉우리마다
대한의 넋이 서리고
백의민족 가슴마다
독립의 얼이 영글어 갑니다

대한 독립 만세
대한의 넋이요
민족의 얼이외다.

만세를 부르던 그 날

만세를 부르던 그 날
1919년 3월 1일
백의민족 흰옷 입고
손에 손에 태극기 들고
대한 독립 만세 함성의 소리
산천초목도 하늘의 별들도 함성의 소리되어
만세를 불렀나이다

북극성의 가장 큰 별은 유관순의 별인가
독립의 외친 소리 별빛이 되었나
태극기 삼천리강산을 뒤덮을 때
북극성 별빛은 더욱 찬란해
민족의 가슴에 애국혼 심어놓았네

서울의 탑골공원 아우내 장터
대한독립 만세의 함성

그곳에 비추어진 별빛되어
조국 강산을 밝히는 봉화되었네

유관순의 별 북극성의 별빛
비추이는 곳마다
애국혼을 심어놓았네.

아우내 장터

천안 삼거리 삼십 리 길 더 가
병천 아우내
사방 골짜기 물이 아울러 만난다고 아우내라 했듯
동서남북 사람들 아우르듯 장날이 서는 곳 아우내

그날은 태극기 아우르듯 모여들었다
물길 모이듯
흰옷의 무리 태극기 무리
모두가 모였네

드디어 터졌다.
대한 독립 만세의 함성
물길 막는 제방처럼 쌓고 쌓은 일제 통치의 뚝도 무너져내린 그 날
태극기 물결인가 만세의 함성인가 백의민족의 정기였나
터졌다 휩쓸렸다

질렀다 소리 소리
터졌다 함성이
대한 독립 만세

출렁이듯 태극기 깃발
대한독립 만세 소리가 출렁이네

아우내 장터
지금도 모여드는 곳
유관순의 봉화로 아우르듯 모여들어라
유관순의 만세 소리 너를 부른다
열사의 아버지 어머니 총칼에 죽어가며
너를 부른다 그 피가 너를 부른다

대한독립 만세 함성이 너를 부르는 곳
아우내 장터.

순국의 오케스트라 합창

삼천리 방방곡곡에 빨갛도록 피어난 진달래꽃 철쭉꽃
대한 독립 외치다 순국한 핏빛이런가

아 온 누리에 붉게 물들인 아름다움이여
만세 소리 함성에 승화되어
한 맺힌 피의 자국이 되었네
조국 독립을 외치다 토한 피멍울이 되었네

이제 그 피가
떠오르는 태양 빛과 더불어
대한 독립의 밝은 빛이 되리라

조선반도 산하에 붉게 물들인 찬란한 빛이여
노래가 되어 찬양하네
대한 독립을 외치며 합창하네

그렇구나
산하를 뒤덮은 개나리는
방방곡곡에 휘날리는 태극기
관현악의 악기되어
오케스트라 연주가 되었네

천만 오케스트라 합창을 들어 보았는가?
3월
한반도에 울려 퍼지는 독립 만세의 함성의 소리
그것은 온 동포가 부르는 오케스트라 합창

할미꽃도 지팡이 짚고
이번만은 머리 들고 같이 노래하네

대한 독립 만세 대한 독립 만세.

태양의 빛이여 어둠을 물리치고 온 누리를 밝게 비추어라

소리가 들리는가
오케스트라 합창의 소리
대한 독립 만세

유관순이 지휘자
마지막 무대는 서대문형무소
매일 밤 열두 시면 울려 퍼진 오케스트라 합창 소리
민족을 깨우는 소리
독립의 씨알이 움트는 소리

그리고
온 세계 사람들의 잠을 깨우는 소리

지구 구석구석까지 태양 빛 비추어 주듯
자유 평등 만세
소리

합창의 소리
오케스트라 소리

특별출연 – 진달래 철쭉 개나리 할미꽃
출연 – 대한의 산천초목
지휘– 유관순
장소– 대한민국
때– 1919년 3월 1일 정오.

기차 소리

고향 가는 길
칙칙폭폭 기차 타고 달리네
뿜어낸 연기 저 멀리 돌아설 때
목메인 기적소리인가

잃어버린 고향 빼앗긴 조국
그래도 기차는 달리네
고향 찾아 달리네
나라 찾아 달리네

언덕 위 숨이 가쁜가
느린 기차 바퀴 소리 치익칙 포옥 폭
조국 잃은 슬픔인가 한숨인가

다시 빨라지는 기차 소리
칙칙폭폭 칙칙폭폭

젊은이 맥박
고향 찾는 소녀들의 가슴 요동치네

기적소리 고향을 알리는가

만세의 합창이 되었네
독립 만세를 외치는 소리인가
조국 대한 독립을 향해 힘차게 달리네

기적소리 대한 독립 만세
응원가 합창이 되었네

기차는 달리네
고향으로 달리네
삼천리강산 독립을 향해 달리네

달려라
기적소리 높여라.

My Everlasting Beloved

I am sixteen years old.
I have a lover.

I always yearn for my beloved,
She is with me to eternity.

The name is Korea on Korean Peninsula.
She is my lover who will live with me forever.

In your bosom forever,
Enjoying freedom and equality,
I will be with you, my beloved.
I call your name at the top of my voice.

For you, my beloved, I sleep,
For you, my beloved, I walk,

For you, my beloved, I breathe.

Only for you, my homeland, Korea,
I will keep my integrity.
For you alone,
I will sacrifice my body.

Hurray for my country, Korea!

My everlasting beloved,
My beloved country, Korea!

Hurray for Independence of Korea

'Hurray for Independence of Korea'
It echoes all over the world.
To the rhythm of the shout,
Korean flag dances in the sky.

'Hurray for Independence of Korea'
The earth shakes,
Mountains, streams, and trees clap their hands.

'Hurray for Independence of Korea'
The shouting permeates into every bone,
And is etched achingly in every soul.

'Hurray for Independence of Korea'
The sound of surrendering your life
Became the blood of martyrdom.

And like an unending river
It flows in the blood of Korean people.

'Hurray for Independence of Korea'
On every mountain top,
The soul of Korea hovers.
In every heart of the nation,
The spirit of independence ripens.

'Hurray for Independence of Korea'
It is the soul of Korea,
It is the spirit of Korean people.

The Day When We Shouted 'Long Live Korea'

Was March 1st, 1919.

Wearing white clothes that symbolized purity of Korea,

Waving Korean flags in our hands,

We shouted 'Long Live Korea'.

We shouted 'Hurray for Independence of Korea'.

We shouted like roaring mountains, streams, and trees.

Is the biggest star in Polaris Kwan Soon Yu's star?

Has the roaring sound of 'Long Live Korea' become the light of
that star?

When Korean flags covered whole nation,

The light of that star shone more brightly.

Spirit of the nation has been planted in all of our hearts.

At the Ahwoonae marketplace of Byoung—Chun and Tapgol
Park in Seoul,

The roaring chorus of 'Hurray for independence of Korea'
Became the starlight,
And transformed into the beacon that's shining all over the
country.

The starlight of Polaris is Kwan Soon Yu's light.
Wherever it shines,
Patriotic spirit is planted.

Ahwoonae Market

Is about ten mile away from Cheonan three—way intersection.

It was named Ahwoonae

Because several streams flowed toward it and met there.

Aptly named Ahwoonae was also a place

Where people gathered on market days.

They came from east, west, south and north.

On that day, Korean flags gathered there.

As the streams met and flowed together,

Crowd of white—clothed people

And Korean flags gathered together.

At last, it exploded!

Thunderous 'Hurray for Independence of Korea'.

On that day, Japanese reign over Korea fell

Like a dyke that failed to block water.

Was it wave of Korean flags, chorus of 'Long Live Korea', or the

spirit of nation of

white clothed people?

It exploded like sweeping waves of ocean!

The thunderous shouts of

'Hurray for Independence of Korea' rang out.

Waves of Korean flags!

Thunderous waves of 'Hurray for Independence of Korea!'

At Ahwoonae marketplace,

People still gather there.

Let them gather there with Kwan Soon Yu's beacon.

Kwan Soon Yu's 'Long Live Korea' is calling you.

Patriot Kwan Soon Yu's mother and father

Who fell at Japanese guns and swords are calling you!

Their blood is calling you!

Ahwoonae marketplace!

That's the place where shouts of 'Long Live Korea' are calling
you.

Orchestral Chorus of Martyrdom

Red azaleas that bloom all over the country,
Are they symbols of blood shed by those who died while
shouting 'Hurray for Independence of Korea'?

Ah, the beauty of red color all around!
Transcended by chorus of 'Hurray for Independence of Korea',
It became footprint of deep sorrow,
And pool of blood, while shouting 'Independence of Korea'.

Now, that blood will become the beacon of independence of
Korea,
Together with the rising sun.

Radiant light that colors the whole nation red,
Becomes a song.
It sings in chorus, 'Hurray independence of Korea'.

Yes!

Forsythias that cover mountains

And Korean flags that fly all over the country

Become musical instruments and perform orchestral symphony.

Have you ever heard a chorus of ten million?

Month of March,

Chorus of 'Hurray for Independence of Korea' that reverberates

all over the nation

Is orchestral music of people of Korea.

Grandmothers(Pasquefolwer) on canes raised their heads,

And sing together 'Hurray for Independence of Korea'.

Let the Sunlight Overcome Darkness and Shine Brightly

Do you hear the music?

The chorus of orchestra,

'Hurray for Independence of Korea'.

Kwan Soon Yu is the conductor.

The last stage is West Gate Prison,

The orchestral chorus reverberates at midnight everyday.

It is the music that awakens whole nation.

It is the sound of sprouting seed of independence.

And

It is the sound to awaken whole world.

As the sunlight shines on every corner of the world,

'Hurray for freedom and equality' is heard everywhere.

Sound of chorus,

Orchestral music.

Special appearances: azalea, forsythia, and pasqueflower,

And natural scenery of Korea

Conductor: Kwan Soon Yu

Place: Korea

Time: Noon, March 1st, 1919

Sound of Train

On the way to hometown,
A choo—choo train is chugging along.
Puff of smoke fades away into distance.
Is it a choked—up sound of miracle?

Lost hometown, disinherited homeland,
The train is still moving,
Moving toward hometown,
Looking for homeland.

Out of breath on a hill,
Sound of train wheels moving slowly,
chug··· chug··· puff··· puff···
Are they sighs of sorrow over lost homeland?

Sound of train wheels moving faster, now

Chug chug puff puff …

Heartbeats of young men and women who are looking for their
hometown

Are becoming faster.

Is it the sound of miracle to signal news of hometown?

It became a chorus of 'Long Live Korea'.
Is it shout of 'Hurray for Independence of Korea'?
It is moving powerfully toward independence of my homeland.

Sound of miracle, 'Hurray for Independence of Korea',
Became a chorus of cheering.

The train is moving,
Toward hometown,
Toward the whole land of Korea.

Keep moving,
Raise the sound of miracle.

세 번째 묶음

사 명
The Mission

사진 설명 : 이화중·고등학교에 세워진 유 열사의 동상과 기념관, 구내 우물
1915년 4월 이화학교로 전입, 1918년 3월 보통과 졸업, 4월 1일 고등보통과로 진학하였으다. 학교 내 이문회를 통하여 하란사, 박인덕, 신형숙(신줄려), 황애덕, 정신학교 김마리아로부터 독립정신을 키웠다.

사진 설명 : 우리 나라 최초에 세워진 정동교회 (1885년 10월 11일 창립)와 1918년 하란사 여사가 헌납한 최초의 파이프오르간(미국 체류 기간 동안 모여진 성금과 재미 동포들의 후원으로 마련) 오르간 뒤 공간이 유관순의 기도 장소요, 독립운동 문서 및 발간소, 태극기 제작소로 사용되었다.

당시 손정도, 이필주 목사와 박동환 전도사의 설교와 기도로 유관순의 애국열이 불타 올랐다.

필자는 유관순을 기억하며 기도하는 중에 눈물이 쏟아졌다.

사명을 위해 사는 사람

비로소
나도 사명을 가진 사람이 되었습니다

새벽잠을 떨치고 먼저 일어나
청소 빨래 물을 긷고 책을 보는 것도 피곤치 않습니다
대한 독립이라는 사명이 있으니까요

친구들과 즐겁게 지내는 것도
전에 몰랐던 보람을 갖습니다
이것 또한 대한 독립을 위한 사명이 있기 때문이지요

의견이 맞지 않아 다투기도 하고
때로는 모두가 그리워 눈물도 흘리지만
보람을 찾습니다
대한 독립을 위한 사명이 있으니까요

쉬기도 하고 잠도 잡니다
보람찬 아침 햇살을 맞으며 기지개를 켤 때도
심장에 요동치는 대한 독립 사명감에서
힘찬 하루가 시작됩니다

묵상과 기도드리며 정중히 성경을 탐독합니다
내 영혼 구원을 향해 믿음으로 달려갈 때도
대한 독립 맥박 소리 들으며
사명을 향해 달려갑니다

하늘의 하느님이 주신 사명
두 손 모아 감사의 기도를 드립니다
주신 사명 감사합니다.

태극기

정동 예배당 앞 제단 파이프오르간
오르간 뒤 조그만 공간
아무도 볼 수 없는 밀실
그곳이 유관순의 기도 골방이다

삼일운동을 준비하는 기도 장소
독립선언문을 베끼며
애국가를 복사하며
태극기를 그리던 곳

흰 바탕에 검은 먹물 빨간 물감
어울리며 태극기 완성될 때
대한 독립이 이루어진다

백두산이 닳고 동해 물이 마르도록
하느님께서 보살피시는 땅 대한민국
그 누가 뺏을 건가

역사가 그려지듯 태극기 선이 그어진다
선열들의 넋이 춤을 춘다
순국의 얼이 살아난다

태극기 손에 들고 만세 부를 때
태극기도 외친다
선조들의 넋이 소리 지른다
대한 독립 만세
나라를 지켜온 국기

정동 예배당 한 세기 넘게 지켜온 파이프오르간
그 소리 울릴 때마다
유관순의 태극기가 춤을 춘다
소리친다
대한 독립 만세.

대한 독립의 씨알

당신의 순국은 독립의 씨알이 되어
겨레의 가슴에 심어놓은 대한 독립 만세의
영원한 씨알이 되었나이다

씨알은 생명이 있어
저 푸른 하늘 향해 줄기차게 뻗어가리
대한 독립을 외치며
무궁화 무궁화처럼 피어나리

하느님이 내려주신 약속이었기에
새 생명의 씨알이 되었소이다

씨알의 부활을 보나이다
매봉산 봉홧불 타오르는 불꽃 속에
들려오는 대한 독립의 소리
영원을 향해 메아리되어

지금도 겨레의 가슴에 들려오나이다

마구간보다 더 차가운 지하 고문실에서
부활 생명의 씨알이 태어났구나
영원한 대한 독립의 씨알이

그래서 해마다 외치네
영원한 하늘 향해
대한 독립 만세
겨레의 가슴에 겨레의 얼 속에 새겨두리라

씨알이여 영원한 생명의 씨알이여.

애국의 화신 유관순

드높은 하늘
끝없는 수평선은
당신의 애국심인가요

하늘 천둥소리보다 더 우렁찬 대한 독립 만세

옥중 한밤중에도 울려 퍼지는 소리
잔인무도한 고문도 막을 수 없었다지요

하늘에 가득 찬 독립 만세 소리
애국의 화신이 되어 터져나오는 그 소리를 누가 막을 수 있었겠습니까

당신의 애국 화신은
천년만년을 이어갈
민족의 고귀한 얼이 되었나이다

어둠을 물리치는 빛처럼
달을 삼키는 바다 밀물처럼
당신의 화신은 빛이 되었나이다
당신의 태극기는 밀물처럼 밀려온 바다가 되었습니다

천년만년 이어갈 애국의 화신
영원토록 이어갈
민족의 얼이 되었나이다.

나는 대한의 사람

법정신문

이름은, 침묵
유관순 맞는가, 유관순 맞습니다

고향은, 침묵
천안군 동면 용두리 338번지 맞는가, 삼천리 반도가 나의 고향이요
주소입니다

현재 이화여학교 고등과 재학 중인가,
대한 조국이 나의 학교입니다
대한 사람 대한 독립 만세를 부른 것이 무슨 잘못인가
일본 사람이 내 나라에서 재판장이 되어 재판하는
이따위 잘못된 짓이 어디 있는가 나는 해야 할 일을 했을 뿐이다
대한의 사람으로 대한 독립 만세를 부르는 것은
마땅히 해야 할 일 아닌가

그래서
나는 외친다
대한 독립 만세
내가 발 닿는 곳마다 외친다
대한 독립 만세

대한의 하늘
대한의 대지에서
살아도 죽어서라도
오직 대한 독립 만세

무궁화 한 송이 되어
이 강산 저 강산에 피어나듯
소리 한 송이
대한 민국 만세

나는 대한의 사람.

대한 여성의 혼 절개 효성

당신이 가진 혼은 논개의 혼입니까

당신의 절개는 낙화암 궁녀의 절개입니까

당신이 바친 생명의 제물은 심청의 효성이었습니까

혼과 절개 그리고 효성으로
모두어져 외친 한마디
대한 독립 만세

목숨 다하기까지
대한 독립 만세

그 혼과 절개 그리고 효성이
대한 여성의 핏줄을 이어 갑니다

기차의 기적처럼
달릴수록 커지는 멀리 힘찬 소리
대한 독립 만세

긴 역사를 이어가는
대한 여성의 외침
대한 독립 만세
영원히.

나의 신앙 고백 (1)

기억합니다

손정도 목사님 송별 예배 마지막 말씀
그 말씀이 제 신앙 고백이 되었습니다

"의를 위해 핍박을 받을 때 천국의 소유자가 된다
주님의 십자가 죽음이 사람의 죄와 사망에서 구원하시는 제물이 되어
부활과 영생을 주셨다는 말씀
나라의 독립을 위하여 모든 고통과 희생을 각오하며
목회의 길을 떠나신다는 말씀"
눈물을 흘리시며 고별설교를 마치셨지요

기억합니다

나라의 독립을 위한 사명 다하기 위하여
자신을 버릴 각오를 하신 목사님의 위대하신 모습
제 뇌리에서 떠나지 않습니다

목사님의 말씀은 저와 항상 같이 있습니다

말씀이 사람이 되었다
뜻을 가지고 행동하는 사람이 되었다는 말씀이시겠지요
저도 간직한 말씀과 함께 희생과 죽음을 각오합니다

나라 위한 사명이 내게 있다면
저도 주님 가신 길 따르겠습니다

나의 희생이 나라의 독립을 위한 제물이 될 수 있다면
기꺼이 바치리이다

나의 첫 번 신앙 고백입니다
나의 신앙 간증입니다
내가 부를 찬송입니다.

나의 신앙 고백 (2)

새로 부임하신 이필주 목사님 설교

"누가 이 땅의 주인입니까
당신이 이 땅의 주인이라면
이때가 **빼앗긴** 나라의 주권을 찾아야 할 때가 아닙니까

기미년 3월 1일 이 날
대한 나라의 주권을 찾기 위해
독립 만세의 시위가 열릴 것입니다"
주일 아침 예배 설교는
나를 부르는 소리였습니다
이 땅의 주인은
일본인도 중국인도 러시아인 그 누구도 아니다. 될 수도 없다
내가 곧 이 땅의 주인이다
만년 이상 단군의 핏줄을 이어받아
이 땅을 지켜온 백의민족의 후손이기 때문이다

나는 결심합니다
독립 만세 시위에 기필코 참가할 것입니다
주님 능히 목숨까지 바칠 수 있는 각오와 용기를 주시옵소서
행동하는 애국의 용기를 주시옵소서

대한 사람 대한으로 길이 보전하세
백의민족 대한의 후손인 유관순
이 소녀의 신앙 고백 위에
함께해 주옵소서
인류 구원을 위해 십자가를 지신 주님을 바라봅니다
조국을 위해 저도 십자가를 지겠나이다.

나 달이 되고 싶어

캄캄한 밤 오솔길 비춰주는 달빛이 되고 싶어
자기 집 찾아가는 밤 짐승들
엄마 품 그리워 길을 찾는 밤새들
달빛 따라 찾아가겠지

조국 산하 보고 싶어 밤하늘 바라보는
망향의 나그네 애국의 순례자
달 속에 나라 그리며
달 속에 부모님 얼굴 보여줄 수 있다면
나 달빛 영상이 되고 싶어

나라 빼앗긴 깜깜한 조국 하늘 산과 강물
빗물이 눈물 되고 물소리 파도 소리 통곡의 소리
그 소리 들어주는 달이 되고 싶어

빼앗긴 조국
빼앗긴 자유의 빛
깜깜한 조국 한반도
나 홀로라도 달빛되어
자유의 빛을
독립 만세의 횃불을
밝히 비추어 주는
나 달이 되고 싶어.

나의 어머니

나라 위해 목숨 던진 어머니
어머니는 진정 나의 어머니입니다
대한의 어머니입니다

원수를 갚기 위해 외장의 몸을 껴안고
남강의 이슬로 사라진 논개
내 한 몸 던지도록 가르쳤사오니
당신은 나의 어머니입니다
대한의 어머니입니다

대한 여성의 지조를 지키기 위해
낙화암에서 투신한 백제의 궁녀들
나에게도 민족의 지조를 가르쳐
목숨 다하기까지
대한 독립 만세 외치게 했사오니
당신들은 나의 어머니입니다

대한의 어머니입니다

앞치마의 돌을 나르다 못해
몸을 던져 외적을 막은 행주산성의 여인들
나에게도 조국을 위해 몸을 던질 용기를 주었사오니
산성의 여인들이여
당신은 나의 어머니입니다
대한의 어머니입니다.

나 촛불되오리다

조국의 어둠을 밝힐 수 있다면
나 촛불 되오리다

일제의 압제에서
깜깜한 내 조국이 되었다면
내 몸을 사르듯
나 촛불되어
흑암을 몰아내리라

대한 독립 만세

촛불 심지 다 아스러지듯
내 몸 불살라 녹아 없어져도
마지막까지 만세 부르리

조국 산하 밝히는
나 촛불되오리다.

A Woman Who Lives for the Mission

At last,
I too became a woman with mission.

Waking up early in the morning,
House—cleaning, laundry and reading books do not make me
tired,
Because I have a mission to accomplish independence of Korea.

Having good time with friends
Also gives me a feeling of benefit that I never felt before,
Because I have a mission to accomplish independence of Korea.

We have different opinions and arguments,
At times we shed tears longing for each other's company,
But all is worthwhile,
Because I have a mission to accomplish independence of Korea.

Resting or sleeping is a part of my daily routine.

When I stretch my arms to embrace the sunshine

To greet a fruitful new day,

It becomes a day charged with new energy.

All because of the mission that beats in my heart for Korean independence.

I read Bible attentively, meditating and praying.

Earnestly seeking my soul in faith,

Hearing the heartbeats of Korean independence,

I run toward my mission.

A calling given by God,

I give Him thanks with both hands together.

Thank you for the calling.

Taegeukgi, Korean Flag

Behind the pipe organ in the altar of Jeongdong Church,

There is a tiny space,

Not visible to anybody.

That alcove was where Kwan Soon Yu used to pray.

That was the place of prayers for March 1st Independence Movement.

That's the place where the Independence Proclamation was copied,

And our national anthem was copied

And Korean flag was drawn.

When black and red ink on white background

Harmoniously blended,

Korean flag was complete.

Until Mt. Baekdu wears down and East Sea dries up

My homeland, Korea, will be protected by God.

Who dares to take it away from us?

The lines of Korean flag are drawn as if history is recorded.

Forefathers and foremothers are dancing.

Spirit of martyrdom becomes alive.

When we shouted 'Long Live Korea' with Korean flags in our hands,

Even the flag seems to shout, 'Hurray for Independence of Korea'.

The spirits of our ancestors also shouted.

'Hurray for Independence of Korea'.

The Korean flag kept our nation together.

The pipe organ has been preserved for over a century.

Whenever the organ plays,

Spirit of Kwan Soon Yu dances,

And shouts,

'Hurray for Independence of Korea'.

'Long Live My Homeland, Korea'!

Seed of Korean Independence

Your martyrdom became the seed of independence,
The everlasting seed planted deep in our hearts,
Symbolizing long life of independent Korea.

The seed has life.
It will mightily fly high into the blue sky,
Shouting 'Hurray for Independence of Korea'.
It will bloom like everlasting flowers.

Promised by God,
You became the seed of new life.

Seed transforms into resurrection.
In the midst of flame of fire on Maebong Mountains,
Shouts of 'Independence of Korea' echoed into eternity.
Even now, they reverberate in our hearts.

In the basement torture chamber colder than stables,

The seed of resurrection was born.

The seed of eternal independence of Korea.

So, every year we shout into the eternal sky,

'Hurray for Independence of Korea'.

Our hearts and our souls will remember it to eternity.

Seed, Seed of eternal life!

Kwan Soon Yu, the Embodiment of Patriotism

High sky,
Endless horizon of ocean,
Do they symbolize your patriotism?

'Hurray for Independence of Korea,
The sound is louder than thunder in the sky.
The sound that reverberated even in prison at midnight,
Even the cruelest torture could not stop it.

'Hurray for Independence of Korea'
The sound of patriotism reincarnated filled the sky.
Who could stop it?

Your patriotic reincarnation
Became holy soul of our nation
That would last thousand and ten thousand years.

Like the light that defies the dark,

Like the ocean waves that swallow moon,

Your patriotic embodiment became the light.

Your Korean flag became an ocean that surged with rising waves.

As patriotic reincarnation

That will last thousand and ten thousand years,

You became the soul of our nation that would exist forever.

I Am Korean

At court hearing,

Your name? Silence
Is your name Kwan Soon Yu? Yes, that is my name.

Where were you born? Silence.
Is 338 Yongdoo Ri, Dong Myun, Chunahn Koon your address?
Korean Peninsula is my hometown and my address.

Are you attending Ewha Girls' School? My homeland, Korea,
is my school.

What's wrong for Koreans to proclaim 'Hurray for
Independence of Korea?'
What's wrong is that a Japanese becomes a judge in my
own homeland and is presiding over a trial. I did what I was

supposed to do. It is my duty as a Korean to declare 'Hurray for Independence of Korea'.

So,
I shout,
'Huray for Independence of Korea.'
I shout wherever my step leads me.
'Huray for Independence of Korea.'

To the sky of Korea,
Land of Korea,
Whether alive or dead,
I will shout 'Hurray for Independence of Korea'.

I will become Moogoonghwa, a rose of sharon
Blooming on mountains of my homeland.,
As a song coming out of a rose of Sharon,
I will shout,
'Long Live Korea'.
I am a Korean.

Soul of Korean Woman, Integrity, Filial Piety

Is your soul that of Nongae?
Is your integrity that of royal maid of honor at Nakhwaam
Rock?
Is your sacrifice of life the filial love of Shimchung?

Cry of soul, integrity, and filial piety combined,
'Hurray for Independence of Korea'.

Until the end of my life,
'Hurray for Independence of Korea'.

The same soul, integrity, and filial piety
Will continue in blood of Korean women.

Like whistle of train,
Distant sound becomes louder as train picks up speed.

'Hurray for Independence of Korea'.

The cries of Korean women that will continue the long history,
'Hurray for Independence of Korea'.
Forever.

Confession of My Faith (1)

I remember,
The last words of farewell sermon by Reverend Jung Do Sohn.
It became confession of my faith.

"Those who are persecuted for justice will inherit the kingdom
of God.
Christ became offering for our salvation,
His Death on the cross and subsequent resurrection
Gave us eternal life.
For independence of Korea,
All pains and sacrifice should be endured."
The last sermon Reverend Sohn delivered with teary eyes still
reverberates.

His determination to achieve Korean independence and
willingness to sacrifice his own life for that goal still echoes in

my ears.

His sermon will always stay with me.

Word became person.

Do you mean a person who has purpose?

Person who acts to achieve that purpose?

I am also determined to sacrifice my life

And willing to face death to achieve that goal.

If I am given the mission for my homeland,

I will follow the path Christ chose.

If my sacrifice could be offering for independence of Korea,

I am willing to give my life.

It is the first confession of my faith.

It is a testimony of my belief.

It is the praise that I am going to sing.

Confession of My Faith (2)

Sermon by newly appointed pastor, Piljoo Lee

"Who is the owner of this land?
If you are the owner,
Isn't it now time to reclaim your ownership?

On March 1st, 1919
This day,
There will be a protest to reclaim sovereignty of Korea,
Demonstration of 'Long Live Independence of Korea'.

The sermon on that Sunday
Was a calling for me.
The owner of my homeland cannot be Japanese, Chinese or
Russian.
I am the owner of my homeland.

Because blood of Dangun, the founding father of Korea ten thousand years ago,
Still flows in me,
And I am a descendant of the white-clothed Korean people,
Who protected their homeland.

I have determined.
I will participate in the 'Hurray for Independence of Korea' demonstration.

Lord, may you grant me courage and determination to willingly risk my own life,
Grant me courage to act for love of my homeland.

May God protect Korean people in Korea forever!
May all remember the confession of faith by Kwan Soon Yu,
A descendant of Koreans, people of white clothes.
Looking up to Christ who had to carry the cross for our salvation,
I, too, will carry the cross for my homeland.

I Wish to Become a Moon

I wish to become the moonlight that illuminates dark trail.
Night creatures that are on the way to their nests,
And birds that are longing to cuddle up in their mothers' arms,
Are on the way to their destination by moonlight.

Patriotic pilgrims and homesick wanderers
Look up to the sky,
Longing to see their homeland!
If I could show reflections of their parents on the moon
I wish to become those images on the moon.

I wish to become the moon
That can hear the laments of the stolen homeland in the dark,
And wails of our sky, mountains, rivers.
And sound of rain that became tears,
And sound of water and ocean waves that became wails.

I wish to become the moon that can hear them all.

My stolen homeland.
The robbed freedom.
The dark Korean peninsula ···
I wish to become the moonlight
That casts a flame of beacon of freedom on my homeland
And a torch of independence.

My Mother

My mother who sacrificed her life,   *
You are truly my mother.
You are the mother of Korea.

Non Gae who disappeared as dewdrops of Nam River
Holding the Japanese general in her arms to revenge!
You taught me to give up my life for the country.
You are my mother.
You are the mother of Korea.

The court ladies of Baekjae Kingdom
Who threw themselves over Nakhwaahm
To uphold principles and beliefs of Korean women!
You taught me to uphold beliefs of our people
And let me shout 'Hurray for Independence of Korea'
Until I take my last breath.

You are my mother.
You are the mother of Korea.

Women of Haengjusan Fortress
Who threw themselves away to defend their homeland
When they could not carry stones in their aprons any longer!
You are my mother.
You are the mother of Korea.

Let Me Be a Candlelight

If I can lift away the darkness of my homeland,
Let me be a candlelight.

If my country became dark
Because of the Japanese oppression,
I will be a candlelight
That lifts the darkness away.

'Hurray for Independence of Korea.'

As candle wick crumbles to pieces
Let my body burn and melt.
Still, I will shout to the last breath, 'Long Live Korea.'

Let me be the candle
That lights mountains and streams of my homeland!

네 번째 묶음

고통과 죽음의 갈림길에서

At the Crossroad of Suffering and Death

서대문형무소

여 옥사 내부

벽 고문실

지하 독방

사진 설명 : 유관순이 갇혀 있던 서대문형무소 : 밤 12시마다 '만세'를 불렀다고 고문을 당하고 벽 고문실 좁은 공간에 갇혀 있어야 했다. 1920년(18세) 9월 28일 감옥에서 순국하였다. 사인은 방광 파열. 10월 14일 정동교회에서 김종우 목사 집례로 장례식 거행하다.

고문 도구/ 쇠를 달구는 화로는 보이지 않는다.

고문 현장 (고춧가루를 코에 넣기)

유관순의 목숨

재판을 받던 날 판사 앞에서

"내 목숨이 하나인 것이 안타깝다
두 개 세 개가 더 있으면
그 목숨 다해 내 나라의 독립을 위해 바치겠다"

울부짖던 당신
대지가 귀 기울이고
하늘이 들었나이다

드디어
당신의 목숨이 끊어진 날
삼천리강산 모두 깜깜한 밤이 되었나이다

그런데
당신의 음성을 들은 대답인지

저 하늘 끝에서 별 하나 떠오르더니
점점 별들로 하늘에 가득 찹니다

분명
당신의 넋이 별이 되어
당신의 목숨으로 가득 찼습니다

삼천리강산
밤하늘 가득한 별빛은
당신의 넋입니다
당신의 목숨입니다

당신의 뜻이 이루어졌나이다

분명
대지가 귀 기울이고
하늘이 들었기 때문입니다.

나를 지키시는 하느님

감옥
차가운 겨울밤
뼈까지 얼어붙는 감방
그래도
견딜 수 있었나이다
대한 조국이라는 대지가
나를 품고 있었기 때문이지요

앉을 공간도 없는 좁디좁은 독방일지라도
나는 견딜 수 있었나이다
대한 조국 하늘이
나의 지붕이 되어 있었기 때문이지요

시뻘건 쇠꼬챙이로
찌르고 지져도
나는 아프지 않았나이다

영원토록 불변하는
내 속 대한 조국의 얼
영원한 생명 씨알을
하느님이 지켜주시기 때문이지요

하느님이 보우하사
우리나라 만세

영원히
나를 지키시는 하느님.

생명 탄생

감옥은 죽음인가
철창 속 손발이 묶이고
입에는 자갈
본능의 자유마저 빼앗긴 곳

그런데
칠흑 같은 죽음 속에서
새 생명이 탄생하였다
죽음의 적막을 깨뜨리는 소리
생명의 울음소리다

그 누구도 막을 수 없는 새 생명의 탄생
생명은 하느님의 섭리
그 누가 거스르랴

생명은 자란다

엄마의 젖을 빨면서
배설도 하면서

차가운 감옥에서 아기가 울 때
얼음과 같은 아기 기저귀
내 가슴에 품어 그 열기로 말린다
그것은 생명을 품는 것
대한 조국을 품는 것

대한 독립 새 생명의 탄생이다
내 가슴에서 태어나는 대한 독립이다
뜨거운 가슴에서 분출하는 뜨거운 피
대한 독립 만세

밤 12시 터져나오는 대한 독립 만세
아기 울음소리도 대한 독립 만세.

고독의 제물

열 살 되기 전 집을 떠났습니다
학업을 위해 집을 떠나 고독을 배웁니다
공주에서 일 년 서울 이화에서 사 년

태극기를 들고 독립 만세를 부를 때
외경의 총칼에 부모를 잃고 고아가 되었습니다

감옥 철창에서 더욱 혹독한 고문의 고독을 익혔습니다
매일 밤 12시 독립 만세를 외쳤다고
동료와 헤어져 누울 수도 없는 지하 독방에 갇혔습니다

태양 빛도 없는 깜깜한 지하 감방
이 또한 고독의 시련입니까

감시하는 새빨간 눈초리
고문하는 쇠사슬, 말 신의 막대기채찍 지지는 인두,

고춧가루물 긴 장화 구둣발
몽둥이 바늘 손깍지 끼우는 쇠젓갈
거꾸로 매다는 천장 몽둥이 쇠갈고리 등
외로운 나에게 친구가 되었습니다

이것이
외로움의 훈련입니까
고독의 형장입니까

성경 말씀이 떠오릅니다
주님 십자가에 달릴 때
따르던 무리 제자들 모두 떠났을 때

주위에 있는 것들은
채찍 가시관 쇠망치 세 개의 못 로마군의 창과 칼 신 포도주
돌을 던지는 군중 침을 뱉는 조롱꾼들

그리고 양쪽의 강도 두 명
그래도 통곡하는 여인들이 있었나이다

지금
나를 위해 울어줄 사람도 없는 마지막 고독의 슬픔을 간직한 채
끝내 눈을 감습니다

비로소
십자가에 달리신 주님을 바라봅니다
고독한 주님의 눈동자를 진정 보았습니다

"마음이 가난한 자
의를 위해 핍박을 받는지
하늘나라가 너희 것이다"
주님의 음성을 들었습니다

주님, 십자가 위에서 외로이 일곱 말씀하시고
"다 이루었다." 하셨는데
저도 이때 다 이루었다고 고백할 수 있을까요
용기 있게 대한 독립 만세
다 이루었다고 말할 수 있게 하소서

주님
고독한 내 영혼을 받아 주소서.

한 맺힌 씨알

나라를 빼앗기고
국민의 주권을 빼앗긴 원통
억울하고
분하고
그것이
한 맺힌
씨알이 되었습니다

그 씨알
땅속에 묻혀
밟히고 밟히었더니
드디어
그 씨알이 터져
민족의 얼이 되었나이다
백성의 혼이 되었나이다

나라 위한 눈물 땀 피
영롱한 빛
조국의 영광이려니
민족의 향기이려니

겨레의 가슴속에 간직하여라
자유와 평화의 얼이 되어
영원히 간직하여라.

이 한 몸 조국을 위한 제물이 된다면

내 몸의 끝날이 죽음이라면
이 몸은 언젠가 죽음을 위한 것

조상 선열들의 흘린 피와 땀이 물이 되었고
죽어 묻힌 살과 뼈가 흙이 된 나의 조국 산하
내가 그 물을 마시고
흙 속의 열매로 나의 몸 이루었으니
나의 이 몸은 나라의 몸이 아닌가

이 한 몸을 바쳐
나의 조국 대한 독립 만세를 부를 수 있다면
이에 더한 보람이 어디 있으랴

나의 조국
강토여 옥토여

이곳에
씨알 하나 죽어
천 배 만 배 생명의 씨알을 거두리라.

먼저 그 나라와 그 의를 구하라

그 나라는 하느님의 나라
그리고 우리나라 대한이 아닙니까

그 의란 주님이 우리의 구원자시오
조국의 독립은 하느님의 뜻이며
우리에게 주신 사명이다 확신합니다

주신 사명 위하여
대한 독립을 위하여
이 목숨 바치겠습니다

전지전능하신 하느님
모세와 엘리야에게 주셨던 능력을
내게도 주옵소서

어떤 고문과 형벌에도 굴하지 않고

이길 수 있는
믿음의 능력을 내게도 주옵소서

칼에 찔린 상처가 더 아파옵니다
모진 고문에 방광이 터졌습니다
온몸에 독이 퍼져 살이 부어오르고 썩어가고 있습니다

숨을 거둘 때까지
대한 독립 만세를 부를 수 있는
믿음의 힘을 더해 주소서

정신이 혼미해집니다
목숨 다하기까지
대한 독립 만세 계속 외치게 하소서
대한 독립 만세.

독방

밤 12시
대한 독립 만세
다시 끌려간 지하 고문실
천장에 달아매어 몽둥이로 쇠꼬챙이로
실신한 몸 찬물 뒤덮어
질질 끌어 옆 독방 발길로 쳐넣는구나

추운 겨울
젖은 옷이 뻣뻣이 얼어붙는데
누울 수도 없는 독방
쪼그리고 앉았다 일어섰다

팔도 벌릴 수 없어
뱅뱅 돌다 어지러워 거꾸로 돌고
겨우겨우 돌다 돌다 쓰러져
창가에 스며드는 아침 햇살

날이 밝아오나 보다

깡통 두 개
큰 것은 배설통
작은 것은 밥통
발에 채어 이리저리 뒹굴다
닷새 지나 내 동무가 되었네.

개미

실신해 들어온 독방
내 손잔등에 개미 한 마리
동무로 찾아왔나 간수로 찾아왔나

손바닥 콩밥 부스러기
입에 물고 어디론가 가더니

저녁에 또 찾아왔네
이번에는 세 마리
대한 독립 만세
소식을 가져왔나

나 아파 죽어가는데
너는 아프지 마라, 죽지 마라
태극기 놓지 마라
외쳐라, 대한 독립 만세

너는 볼 거야 들을 거야
독립의 그날
삼천만 겨레 함성의 소리
대한 독립 만세 소리.

나 아파

월터 학장 유우석 오빠 김현경 친구
면회실
부축받아 겨우 면회실로
그토록 기다리던 사람
인사드릴 기운조차 없어
겨우 한마디
나 아파 오빠
퉁퉁 부어오른 몸뚱이
잡은 손 잔등에 연붉은 피가 밴다

나 아파

온몸이 아파
어제도 오늘도 밤에도 낮에도
앉아도 누워도 서도 아파
머리도 사지도 온몸이 다 아파

아파 아파
나라도 아파 백성도 아파

대한 독립 만세 소리
아픔의 소리인가

아파
삼 일 되던 날
숨이 졌다지
죽음도 아파.

* 유관순 열사의 사인 – 방광 파열

거룩한 상처

태극기 장대를 내려친 칼
떨어진 태극기를 사무라이 칼이 찢었다

찢어진 태극기 부둥켜안고
대한 독립 만세 외치는데
사무라이 칼날인가
내 옆구리를 찔렀다

피범벅이 된 저고리
태극기에서 피가 흐른다

대한 독립 만세
쓰리고 아픈 절규인가

피로 물들인 삼천리강산
조국의 강토에 피가 흐른다

고통의 신음 소리 승화되어
뿜어 오르는 핏발이
외치는 만세 함성이 되었구나

상처
거룩한 분노처럼 거룩한 상처

숨 거둘 때까지
아픔의 고통을 주었건만

나 자랑스러운 애국의 흔적을
하늘나라까지 간직하리라
상처 안은 태극기와 같이.

Life of Kwan Soon Yu

On the day of trial,
In front of judge,

"I am sorry I have only one life,
If I have two lives, three lives
I will dedicate all for independence of my country."

You cried,
The earth and sky heard you.

Finally,
When you took your last breath,
Night fell over the whole land of Korea.

Then,
A star appeared on the horizon of sky,

As if it heard your cries.
Gradually the sky was filled with numerous stars.

Clearly,
Your soul became the star
That was filled with your life.

The light of stars
That shined all over whole land of Korea
Is your soul
And your life.

Your mission has been accomplished.

Surely,
The earth listened,
And the sky heard.

God Who Watches Over Me

Prison,

Bitterly cold winter night,

Prison cell where even bones froze.

Yet

I was able to overcome them all

Because my homeland, Korea, embraced me in her bosom.

In a tiny prison cell,

Where there was no space to sit down,

I was able to overcome them all

Because my homeland, Korea, gave a roof over me.

With red and hot iron,

I was poked to oblivion,

Yet I did not feel pain.

Because God watched over

The unchanging spirit of Korea in me

And the eternal seed of life.

'Long Live Our Nation',

May the providential protection be with us!

Forever,

May God watch over us.

Birth of Life

Is prison death?
It is a place of barbed wires
And handcuffs.
It is a place where pebbles are pushed into mouth,
It is a place where even freedom of instincts is forfeited.

Yet,

From death as black mud
Arose a new life.
The sound that broke silence
Is the cry of a new life.

Nobody can prevent birth of new life.
Life is God's providence.
Who dares to defy it?

Life grows,
Suckling at mother's milk,
And excreting, too.

When baby cries in bitterly cold prison,
Mother puts icy cold diapers in her bosom
And dries them with her body warmth.
It is an act of embracing life,
Like embracing my homeland, Korea.

Independence of Korea is birth of a new life.
It is born out of my passionate heart
That is spewing warm blood for motherland.
'Hurray for Independence of Korea'.

At midnight,
Shouts of 'Hurray for Independence of Korea.'
Even babies seem to cry out, 'Hurray for Independence of Korea.'

Offering of Solitude

I left home before I became ten years old.
I learned solitude when I left home to study,
One year in Gongju, four years at Ewha in Seoul.

While I was crying out 'Long Live Korea', waving Korean flag,
I lost my parents to Japanese police, And became an orphan.

I became accustomed to solitude of harsh tortures in prison cell.
Because I shouted 'Hurray for Independence' every midnight,
I was put into solitary confinement in a tiny basement prison cell.

A dark basement prison cell with no sunlight,
Is this also a trial of loneliness?

Red eyes that were watching over me,
Torturing iron chains, wooden sticks, searing hot irons, water

with red pepper powder, long leather boots, iron bars that
locked fingers together, ceiling to hang me upside down, spindle
of iron thread…
They all became my friends.

Is this training of solitude?
Or is it an execution ground of solitude?
I remembered Bible verses:

169

When Jesus was on the cross,
When all of His disciples left,
What's left around Him were

Crown of thorns, iron hammer, three nails, Roman soldiers'
spear and sword,Sour wine, unruly crowd that threw stones at
Him, spitting mockers, And two robbers on each side.

Still, there were women who wept.

Now,
Since there is no one who can cry for me,
I am colsing my eyes,
With last and lonely sadness in my heart.

At last,
I look up the Lord hanging on the cross.
I truly see the eyes of the lonely Jesus.

'Blessed are the poor in spirit,
Blessed are those who hunger, and thirst for righteousness,
For theirs is the kingdom of heaven'
I heard the voice of the Lord.

Lord, you said "it is finished" after seven last words on the cross.

Do you think I also can say 'it is finished' now?

Help me be able to say 'Hurray for independence of Korea. It is finished' courageously.

Lord,

Please take my lonely soul!

Seed with Deep Rooted Grief

Bitter resentment when nation robbed,

And rights of people taken away,

And injustice,

And anger,

All these became a seed of deep—rooted grief.

That seed was buried in soil

And trampled over and over again.

At last,

It burst,

And became the soul of my country.

It became the soul of my people.

Tears, sweat, and blood shed for my country

And a bright light,

All became glory of my homeland

And fragrance of my people.

May the spirit of freedom and peace
Be kept in the hearts of my people!
Forever!

If I Can Give My Body As a Sacrificial Offering for My Country

If the last day of my body means death,
I am always ready for it.

The blood and sweat my forefathers shed became water of my homeland,
Their buried flesh and bones became soil of this land.
I drink that water,
And my body sustains life from what's reaped from that soil.
So, the owner of my body is my homeland.

If I can shout 'Hurray for Independence of Korea'
By sacrificing my body,
Is there anything that is worthier?

My country
My homeland, fertile land!

In this land,

A seed sacrificed

Will reap myriad of seeds of life.

Seek Ye First Kingdom of God and His Righteousness

The nation belongs to Kingdom of God.
That nation is Korea.

I believe
The Lord is our Savior,
Independence of Korea is God's will,
And He gave us the mission to accomplish it.

For that mission,
And independence of Korea,
I will give my body as offering.

Almighty God,
May you grant me the same ability
You gave Moses and Elijah.

May you grant me strong faith

That will sustain my courage not to succumb to

Tortures and harsh punishment.

Stab wound is getting more painful,

My bladder has burst due to harsh tortures.

My whole body is poisoned, swollen, and decomposing.

May you, my Lord, grant me the power of faith

So, I can shout 'Hurray for Independence of Korea'

Before I take my last breath!

I am becoming delirious now.

Until I take my last breath,

Let me shout 'Hurray for Independence of Korea'!

'Hurray for Independence of Korea'!

Solitary Cell

Midnight

'Hurray for Independence of Korea'

I was taken to the torture chamber in basement again,

Hung from ceiling,

Tortured by club and iron skewer,

Splashed with cold water,

Dragged and kicked into next solitary cell.

Bitterly cold winter,

Wet clothes were frozen stiff,

A tiny cell where I could not even lie down,

I squatted and stood up.

Not enough space to stretch my arms,

Turning around and around

I became dizzy and fell.

Morning sunlight through window let me know
Another day dawned.

Two cans;
One for excretion,
A small one for rice.
They were kicked around this way and that,
And they became my friends after five days.

Ant

I must have fainted and now I am in solitary confinement.
I see an ant on my hand.
Is it visiting me here as a friend or a guard?

It went somewhere
With crumbs of rice and beans in its mouth.

It came back in the evening.
There are three of them now.
Did they bring the news of Korean independence?

I am dying with pain.
You shouldn't get sick or die.
Don't put the Korean flag down.
Shout 'Hurray for Independence of Korea'.

You will see and hear,

On the day of independence,

Roaring shout of thirty—million Korean people.

'Hurray for Independence of Korea'.

I Am in Pain

Dean Walter, my brother Ohseuk, and my friend, HyunKyung Kim
Were in the visitor's room.
Assisted, I entered the room.
I missed them very much.
Yet, so exhausted, I was not able to say hello to them.
'I am in pain' was all I could whisper.
Swollen body,
Back of my hand that was held was pink with blood stains.

I am in pain.

My whole body aches.
Yesterday, today, at night, and during day, too.
It aches when I am sitting, lying down, and standing.
My head hurts, my whole body is in pain all over.

I am in pain. I am in pain.

My country is in pain, my people are in pain.

Sound of 'Hurray for Independence of Korea,

Is it sound of moaning in pain?

Aches and pains.

On third day,

She expired.

Even death is painful.

*Cause of death—ruptured bladder

Holy Scar

The sword that hit the Korean flag pole.
The sword of Samurai that tore the fallen Korean flag.

When I hugged the torn Korean flag in my arms,
Shouting 'Hurray for Independence of Korea',
The sword of Samurai was thrusted into my ribs.

My jacket was covered with blood,
The Korean flag was dripping with blood.

'Hurray for Independence of Korea'
Bitter and painful scream!

Whole land of Korea was stained with blood.
Now that blood is flowing in rivers and soaked in soil of my
motherland.

Moaning of pain that was transcended

And sound of blood that was gushing out

Became the roar of 'Long Live Korea'.

Until my last breath,

However painful it might be,

I will proudly cherish love for my nation,

Together with the torn Korean flag.

기도와 용서

Prayer and Forgiveness

사진 설명 : 매봉산 정상에 세운 유관순 열사의 초혼묘
(유 열사의 장지는 이태원 공동묘지로 되어 있으나 찾지 못하고 있다.)

유관순의 용서

나라를 빼앗고
백성을 노예로 부리던 일본 제국
나의 애국심을 짓밟고
삼천리 강토를 탈취한
제국의 악귀들을 용서할 수 있을까

끝없는 하늘에 가득 채워진 만행을
어떻게 지을 수 있을까
새벽마다 통곡하는 바다의 파도 소리가 들리는가

용서
영혼의 소리인가 주님의 음성인가
네가 하는 것이 아니다
내가 하는 것이다

십자가 고통 속에서도

저들을 용서하신 주님
주님만이 할 수 있음을 깨달았습니다

용서하라
7번에서 70까지라도 용서하라 하신 주님

원수도 없고 고통도 없는 하느님 나라에서
용서가 무엇인지
비로소 알았습니다.

마지막 기도

십자가 바라봅니다
인류 구원의 완성이었기에
그것은 하느님의 마지막 일이었나요

나도
대한 조국을 위한
마지막 제물이 되어지기를
기도드립니다

그러나
주님의 뒤를 따르던 제자들 순례자들이 남겨놓은 십자가를 보았습니다
그것이 곧 생명의 씨알임을 깨달았습니다
영생의 씨알

대한 독립 만세
그것 또한 씨알이 되어

삼천리 강토에 피어나는 무궁화처럼
영원토록 피어나게 하소서.

Forgiveness of Kwan Soon Yu

Japanese empire stole my country,
And took Korean people as its slaves,
And trampled my patriotism,
And took the whole land of Korea,
Would I be able to forgive its evil acts?

How could I forgive its countless atrocities?
Do you hear wailing sound of ocean waves every dawn?

Forgiveness …
Is it voice of my soul or voice of the Lord?
"Forgiveness is not done by you,
But by me", the Lord says.

Suffering so much pain on the cross,
You still forgave us.

I realize, my Lord, you are the only one who can pardon us.

Forgive.

Lord, you told us to forgive 7 times and even 70 times.

In the kingdom of God where there are no enemies or no pains,
I have finally realized what forgiving is all about.

Last Prayer

I look up to the cross.
It completed the salvation of humanity.
Was it God's last work?

I pray I too would be the last offering
For my homeland, Korea.

But,
I saw the cross that Jesus' disciples and pilgrims left.
I realized it was a seed of life.
The seed of eternal life!

'Hurray for Independence of Korea'
May this shout also become seed
And bloom eternally,
Like mugunghwa flowers that bloom on my homeland, Korea.

여섯 번째 묶음

편지
A Letter

매봉교회

유관순 생가

매봉산 정상을 향한 길 : 길을 따라 시가 새겨진
석비가 놓여 있다.

사진 설명 : 유관순 어렸을 때 다녔던 매봉교회 가까운 곳에 유 열사의 생가가 있다. 집 뒷산의 매봉산으로 거사
전날 밤 봉홧불을 유 열사가 직접 올린 곳이다. 산 정상을 따라 이화 학생들의 열사를 기리는 시가 돌에 새겨져
양 옆으로 20여 점이 있다. 열사에게 보내는 편지인 동시에 우리에게 보내는 열사의 혼이 담긴 편지이기도 하다.

순국하신 아버님 어머님께

나를 낳아주시고 길러주신 부모님
공주로 서울로 유학을 보내주셨지요
학자의 가문에서 선진 개혁의 눈을 뜨게 하시고
나라 사랑을 일깨워주신 아버지
나에게 기독교 신앙을 갖게 하신 어머니 할아버지 삼촌
아우내 장터 독립 만세 시위에서 부모님이 순국하실 때
나는 하늘이 무너지는 것 같았습니다

사지가 떨리는 울분에 죽을 각오로 왜경에 달려들었습니다
놈들의 칼이 내 옆구리를 찔렀으나
아랑곳없이 맨손으로 총부리를 막으며
대한 독립 만세를 외쳤습니다
재판을 받을 때도 감옥살이할 때도
부모님 순국하신 영상이 항상 떠올랐습니다
빼앗긴 나라를 생각할 때 울분을 금치 못했습니다
그러나 하느님

감옥에서 일 년 이상 온갖 악형을 받고
마지막 방광이 터져 온몸에 독이 퍼져 숨이 막히고 정신이 혼미해질 때
비로소 깨달았습니다

먼저 하늘나라에 가신 부모님께서
나라를 위하여 기도하시며
제가 있을 주님 나라의 자리를 준비하고 계시다라는 것을 알겠습니다
부모님 기도하신 대로
두 분의 뒤를 용감히 따르겠습니다

천년만년 이어갈 독립의 혼을 이어받고
보람토록 자손만대 계승할 수 있게 하셨으니 감사합니다
부모님 먼저 순국하신 것도 하느님의 섭리셨던가요
살아있는 애국자보다 목숨 바친 애국자
그 값이 더 귀하다는 것을
이제 알고 확신하게 되었습니다
아버님 어머님 감사합니다

 딸 유관순 올림
 1920년 10월 12일 숨지기 직전

하늘나라에서 온 편지

바람 없는 하늘나라에서도
대한 독립 만세
아직도 제 손에 태극기가 휘날리고 있습니다

천사들의 노랫소리
그것 또한 만세 소리입니다

하느님 손길 대한민국을 감싸 안으신 손길
여기 하늘나라에서 봅니다

한 겨레가 만년을 간직해온 대한
"하느님이 보우하사 우리나라 만세"
"동해 물이 마르도록 백두산이 닳도록"
돌보아 주신 그 손길 사랑의 손길
나는 보고 있습니다

슬픔 외로움 고통 욕심 미움도 없는 곳
모두 한 가족 하느님의 자녀
모두 하느님의 사랑을 받고 있습니다

자유 평등이 공존하는 곳
영생의 세계

우렁차게 우렁차게
대한 독립 만세
천군 천사들이 손뼉을 칩니다.

천국에서 온 편지 (2)

하느님의 뜻을 따라
나라의 독립을 위하여
이 한 생명 바칠 수 있었으니
하느님께 감사와 영광을 바칩니다

동포여 세계인이여
하느님의 사랑이 무엇인지
믿음을 가지고 사십시오

악을 따르다 지옥의 형벌을 받지 말고
주님의 뒤를 따라
의의 길에서
생명의 참된 가치를 깨닫고
주님을 위해 나라 위해
그 생명 바치어
나와 같이 하늘나라 백성이 되기를 기도드립니다

이제 내가 하느님 나라에서 하느님의 딸이 되었으니
자유 평등 진리의 봉화를 들고
어두운 세상을 밝히리라.

To My Father and Mother Who Sacrificed Their Lives for Korea

My parents, who brought me into this world,

Sent me to schools in Gongju and Seoul.

My father was from family of scholars.

He opened my eyes to new world of developed countries,

And kindled love for my homeland.

My mother, grandmother, and uncle helped me embrace

Christian faith.

When my parents were martyred during Independence

Movement Demonstration

At the Ahwoonae marketplace,

I felt as if the sky had fallen on me,

And my body shook in anger.

Risking my life, I fought Japanese police.

Japanese police lunged his knife into my side,

Fearlessly I tried to block his gun with my bare hands,

And I shouted 'Hurray for Independence of Korea.'

Even at the court trial and in prison,
I could not help but thinking of my parents.
They sacrificed their lives for Korea.
Whenever I thought about my stolen country,
I could not help but getting angry at the enemy.

But, oh Lord,
After a yearlong torture in prison,
When my body was just about to expire with poison from
ruptured bladder,
I finally realized
My parent who went to be with you
Was preparing my place in heaven,
Still praying for Korean independence.

I understand now.

As my parents prayed,

I will follow their paths courageously.

Succeeding the spirit of independence that will last forever,

I am thankful for that inheritance

That will go on generation after generation.

Was my parents' martyrdom also a part of the God's plan?

I am now convinced

The value of the patriots who sacrificed their lives

Is greater than that of living patriots.

Thank you, mother and father!

      Your daughter, Kwan Soon Yu

      October 12, 1920 (Just before I drew my last breath)

A Letter from Heaven

Even in the windless and calm heaven,
'Hurray for Independence of Korea,'
Korean flag is still flying in my hand.

Angels' singing
Is also 'Long Live Korea'.

From heaven above,
I watch God's helping hand that is embracing the land of Korea,

Korea that has been cherished for ten thousand years!
"May God protect and preserve our homeland!
Hurray for Korea."
I see the God's loving and helping hand on it
"Til the waters of the East Sea run dry and Mt. Baekdu is worn
away."

It is the place where freedom and equality coexist,
The place of eternal life.

Sonorously, loudly
'Hurray for Independence of Korea.'
Myriad of angels are clapping their hands.

A Letter from Heaven (2)

Following God's will,

And for independence of Korea,

I gave my life.

I give thanks and glory to Him.

People of Korea and citizens of the world,

May you live in faith,

Knowing what God's love is all about.

May you not follow evil way and be punished for it,

But follow God's way!

On the path of righteousness,

Realizing the true value of life,

For the Lord, and for our country,

Give your life

And be a citizen of God's kingdom as I did.

Now, I became a God's daughter in the kingdom of God,

I will light up the world

With beacon of freedom, equality, and truth.

애국의 혼
The Spirit of Patriotism

사진 설명 : 병천 아우내 장터에 세워진 독립만세기념탑. 1919년 4월 1일, 이 날 유관순 열사의 부모가 일제의 총칼에 순국하시고 유 열사는 옆구리에 칼의 부상을 입었다.

아우내 만세운동 발생지

3.1독립운동 중 가장 큰 운동이 바로 아우내장터의 만세 시위이며
순국열사의 순국정신은 우리고장의 자랑이며 우리민족의 영구불멸의
귀감이 될 것이다.

당시 거사일로 정한 아우내장날인 1월 1일, 독립선언을 선포키 위하여
3천여명의 군중이 모여 아우내장터가 폭발인데 가장 많은 인파를 이루
었으며, 경찰주재소와 유관순열사께서 군중 앞에 나서서 비장한 연설을
하자 군중들은 일제히 독립만세를 외쳐 불리어 독립운동의 거점이 되어
또한 그때 대한병의 무차별 사격으로 19명의 사상자가 숨을 거두게 되어
발생하고 유관순열사께서도 체포되어 아우내장터의 시위를 끝을 맺었다.

순국사 명단(19명)

애국가

하느님
백두산이 다 닳도록
동해 물이 다 마르도록
한반도 대한을 그토록 사랑하시나요
만년 대계를 지켜주시며
보호하신다고 다짐하신 하느님

대한 사람 대한으로
길이 보전하세
온 동포들의 다짐입니다
하느님께서 주신 사명이지요

한반도 대한을 지킴은 하느님 지킴이요
한반도 대한의 독립은
하느님께서
우리 민족에게 주신 사명 아닙니까

조국을 위해
나 한 몸 바침

하느님 뜻 따름입니다

목청껏 애국가 부르며
나라 위하여
이 한 몸 기꺼이 바치리이다

제 이름은
유관순입니다.

영원히 타오르는 별빛

조국 산하를 찬란케 하는 밤하늘의 별
태양 빛에 별빛은 숨은 건가 감추어진 것인가

태양이 저물 때 떠오르는 별빛
어둠이 짙을 때 더 찬란히 빛나는 별빛이여

별빛 속에 광채 빛나는 빛살
선열의 혼인가 넋인가 얼인가 정신인가

먹물 붓끝에서 빛나는 빛살
휘두른 칼끝에서 번득이는 빛살

광개토대왕의 별
세종대왕의 별
이순신 장군의 별
유관순의 별

영원히 꺼지지 않고 타오르는 별빛

조국을 지키는 등대인가 봉화인가
하느님 사명을 지킨 파수꾼인가

영원히 타오르는 별빛 그 빛살을 본다

조국아 바라보아라, 간직하여라

저 타오르는 별빛 그 찬란한 빛살
이 강토 산하에 겨레 가슴에 영원히 빛나거라.

고난의 순례자

고난의 길
불나방처럼 뛰어들어
밤하늘 별똥의 불빛처럼
온몸을 던져버린 당신

때문에
생명이 타오르는 빛을 봅니다
깜깜한 세상의 빛이 되어
숨겨졌던 대한의 얼을 봅니다

일만 년을 이어갈 씨알이 되어
고난의 길 순례의 길을 걸어가소서

흙 속의 씨알이 벗겨지는 생명처럼
고난의 아픔을 감싸 안으며
영원한 생명을 탄생시켰습니다

민족이 뚫고 나갈
고난의 길을 열어

너무도 아름다운
한 송이 무궁화를 피웠습니다
영원을 노래하는
무궁화를 피웠습니다.

매봉산의 봉화

우리 집 뒷산은 매봉산
개나리 진달래 벗 삼아
동무들과 술래잡기 강강술래 놀던 곳
엄마 따라 산나물 캐어
밥상에는 가득한 봄철 나물로 입맛을 돋우며
즐거움이 가득한 밥상이었지

이제 철들어
매봉산에 오를 때
나는 횃불을 들어 봉화에 불을 붙였다
민족을 깨우는 봉홧불
강산의 정기를 뿜는 봉화의 불이 타오를 때
선조들의 불타는 애국의 불꽃을 보았다

잠자던 얼을 깨우는 불빛
민족의 사명을 깨우는 불길

관창의 애국충정이 묻힌 곳
계백의 기백이 뻗쳐있고
충무공의 애국충정이 서려 있는 이곳
천년만년 이어갈 조국의 생명이 봉화처럼 불탈 때
꺼지지 않는 불길되어
새 생명의 부활을 보여 주리라

불타오르는 봉화
민족아 보아라
민족아 깨어나라
애국 열정의 불길을 높여라

한반도를 밝히고
아시아 그리고 세계를 밝혀라
조선 반도의
영원히 타오르는 봉화를 보아라

대한 독립 만세
만세토록 꺼지지 않는
매봉산 봉화를 보아라.

Korean National Anthem

Dear Lord,
Until Mt. Baekdu wears down,
And the East Sea dries up,
You said you would love Korea.
You promised you would preserve
And protect your grand plan for Korea forever.

Great Korean people
Will stay true to the Great Korean way!
It is a pledge of all Koreans.
It is a mission God gave us.

Protection of Korea on Korean Peninsula
Is God's providence.
Isn't Independence of Korea
A God given mission for Korean people?

For my homeland
I give my life.

It is simply God's plan.

Singing the Korean national anthem to the top of my voice,
For my homeland,
I will sacrifice my life willingly.

My name is
Kwan Soon Yu.

Starlight That Is Burning Forever

The star in the night sky that shines brightly
over mountains and streams of my homeland;
Is it hidden from sunlight or covered by it?

The star that rises after sundown;
It shines brighter when the dark becomes thicker.

The bright beam of light among stars;
Is it soul, spirit, life, or essence of our ancestors?

The light that shines at the tip of black ink brush,
The gleaming light at the tip of swinging sword,
The star of King Kwanggaeto,
Star of King Saejong, general Soonshin Lee, and Kwan Soon
Yu;
Blazing star lights that are burning to eternity.

Are they lighthouses and beacons that watch over my
homeland?
Are they sentinels of God's mission?
I see the rays of starlight that is burning to eternity.

My Dear homeland, Korea,
Keep the lights burning.
Let the lights shine
On mountains and streams of my homeland
And hearts of Korean people.

Pilgrim in Suffering

Path of suffering.
Because you sacrificed yourself
Like a tiger moth,
Like light of shooting star,
We see a bright star full of life.
And we see the hidden soul of Korea
That became the light in the dark world.

May you be a seed that will last to eternity,
May you walk the path of pilgrim triumphantly!

Like life that is coming out of seed in soil,
Embracing pain of suffering,
You gave birth to eternal life.

By opening path of suffering

That our nation has to overcome,

You let a beautiful rose of Sharon bloom,

Mugunghwa that sings a song of eternity.

Beacon of Mt. Maebong

The mountain behind my house is Maebongsan.
Forsythias and azaleas as my friends,
I used to play hide—and—seek and circle dance there.

I used to pick wild edible greens with my mother there.
Our dining table was always full of delicious spring greens.
It was time full of laughter and happiness.

Now I became an adult.
I went up Mt. Maebong with a torch,
And I lit the beacon at the mountain top.
The light of the beacon awakened spirit of our nation.
I witnessed the sparkles of our ancestor's patriotism
As the flame of the nation's energy was afire.

The flame that awakened soul from sleep.

The flame that awakened mission of the country.
The nation where patriotism of Kwanchang is buried,
And spirit of General Gyebaek is ingrained,
And patriotism of Admiral Yi Sun—shin prevails.

When the life of my country that will continue for thousand years
Burns like beacon fire,
Let it be inextinguishable light
And show resurrection of new life!

Burning beacon fire,
May my people witness it!
May my people wake up!
Raise the flame of patriotism!
Let it illuminate Korean peninsula.
Let it light up the whole world.
Look at the eternal flame of the beacon!

'Hurray for Independence of Korea.'
Look at the inextinguishable beacon of Mt. Maebong!

유관순

Kwan Soon Yu

유관순 열사
神魂順殉士
Patriotic Martyr
Yoo, Kwan-sun

사진 설명 : 매봉산 정상, 유 열사가 거사 전날 밤 12시 봉화불을 올린 곳이다. "영월히 불타오르는 별"의
현장이다.

유관순

−대한 독립 만세

유관순을 한 마디의 시로 표현한다면 "대한 독립 만세"이다.

그의 생 전부가 대한 독립 만세였기 때문이다.

유관순 열사가 남겨놓은 시나 편지, 어록 하나도 없다.

그러나 유관순은 대한민국 역사에 길이길이 남을 글을 남겨 놓았다.

그것은 조국의 얼 속에 씨알이 되어 아로새겨 놓은 것이 있으니 곧 대한 독립 만세이다.

도산의 말처럼 밥을 먹어도, 길을 걸어가도 대한 독립이라 했듯이 유관순 역시 공부를 해도, 일을 해도, 친구와 놀이를 해도 대한 독립이었다. 그는 마지막 숨을 거둘 때도 차가운 지하 형무소에서 외친 것이 대한 독립 만세였다. 대한 독립 만세를 불러 재판을 받고 고문을 당하고 인간으로 견디기 어려운 수치, 멸시, 고통을 감수하면서도 끝까지 대한 독립 만세를 외쳤다.

그의 청순한 정신, 얼은 그 어느 누구도 무너뜨리 수 없었다. 뺏을 수 없었다.

오늘 우리들 곧 대한민국 국민이라면 모두 모두 유관순이 외친 대한 독립 만세 소리를 들어야 한다.
지금도 외치는 그 소리를 들어야 한다.
서해 동해 남해의 출렁이는 파도소리도, 금수강산 골짜기마다 들리는 바람소리도, 산촌이나 들판에 새소리도, 노을진 벌판의 송아지 소리도 마을의 짖어대는 개소리도 모두 모두 대한 독립 만세를 외치고 있다.

우리의 넋도, 혼도 귀를 열어 뼛속까지 스며드는 만세 소리가 들리는가 가슴 터질 듯 우렁찬 거레의 함성, 유관순의 소리가 들리는가 대한 독립 만세의 소리

유관순
대한 독립 만세

영원한 그의 비문이요 그의 노래요 한반도에 거룩한 짧은 어록의 시 구절이다.

한반도 배달겨레

대한 독립 만세

Kwan Soon Yu

— 'Hurray for Independence of Korea'
If Kwan Soon Yu can be described in one poetic expression,
It is 'Hurray for Independence of Korea'.
Her whole life existed only for independence of Korea.

There are no poems, letters, or quotations she left behind.
Yet she gave us a legacy that will be remembered throughout
Korean history. She instilled the seed of independence in the
soul of Korean people.

Dosan Ahn Chang-ho said he thought about Korean
independence all the time, even during meals and on his walks.
Kwan Soon Yu also always thought about Korean independence,
while studying, working, and playing with friends. Even when
she was taking her last breath in the cold basement prison cell,
she shouted 'Hurray for Independence of Korea'.

She shouted 'Hurray for Independence of Korea' to the top of her voice at every midnight like timed fountain of lava. The cause of her death was rupture of uterus and bladder according to her death certificate. It was signed by a doctor of the West Gate Police Station. Her body was covered with wounds. Still, she shouted 'Hurray for Independence of Korea'. Nobody could destroy her sincere spirit and pure soul. Nobody could take her determination away.

As Korean citizens, we all have to listen to her shout now, 'Hurray for Independence of Korea'. Sound of waves of West Sea, East Sea, and South Sea; sound of wind from rivers and mountains of Korea; sound of birds in mountain villages and fields; sound of calves on sunset fields; and sound of barking dogs in villages; they all are shouting 'Hurray for Independence of Korea'.

Open your heart, your soul and your ears. Do you hear the shout, 'Long Live Korea' that permeates into your very bones? Among resonating roars of our people, do you hear Kwan Soon Yu's voice? Shout of 'Hurray for Independence of Korea'.

Kwan Soon Yu.

'Hurray for Independence of Korea'

A short poem quoted from her eternal epitaph, her song.

Another new poem has been left.

It is the seed Kwan Soon Yu created from pain of birth.

They are 'Korean People of Korean Peninsula' and 'Last Prayer'. As history of salvation on the cross was the last step in God's salvation for humanity, I want to believe the sacrifice Kwan Soon Yu made for Korean independence is also the last one for her.

Korean People on Korean Peninsula

'Hurray for Independence of Korea'

온 몸이 불덩어리가 되어

이용해 (수필가)

　며칠 전 장철우 목사님의 유관순 시집을 읽어 보아달라는 부탁을 받고 이메일로 보내주신 시를 읽어 내려가기 시작했습니다.

　읽어 내려가면서 가슴이 뜨거워지기 시작했고 목은 막혀 숨조차 쉬기 힘들어지고 내가 시를 읽는 게 아니라 애국자의 절규를 듣는 게 아닌가 하는 생각을 했습니다. 정녕코 이 글은 장미꽃이나 모란꽃을 노래하는 시가 아니라 가슴에서 터져나오는 절규이고 글줄마다 마치 핏자국이 보이는 것 같은 착각을 느꼈습니다. 아마도 시인이 태어나기도 전에 이 세상에 나라사랑의 사명을 갖고 태어났고 공주 영명소학교 이화학당에서 나라사랑의 혼이 영글어 지금부터 97년 전 활활 타버린 민족과 나라 사랑의 혼을 부르는, 소녀를 부르는 시인의 애타는 초혼의 절규였습니다.

　목청을 다하여 부르노라 부르는 소리는 비끼어가고 하늘과 땅 사이가 너무 넓구나 하고 통곡했던 소월의 가슴처럼 유관순 열사를 부르는 시인의 목소리가 하늘의 구름 사이로 번갯불이 비켜 가듯이 구름 사이로 빛 사이로 비켜 가고 있었습니다.

　그러나 시인은 멈추지 않습니다. 그대로 이런 채 돌이 되어도 내가 부를 이름이여 사랑하는 그 이름이여, 라고 멈추지 않습니다. 그리고 46편의 시를 써내려 갑니다.

　시인은 공주 영명학교로 이화학당으로 그리고 유관순 열사가 만세를 불렀다는 병천으로 아우네 장터로 달려 갑니다. 마치도 무엇을 보고 혼이 나간 사람처럼 유관순 누나 유관순 누나 하며 달려갑니다. 그리고는 쓰러져 하나님께 애원을 합니다. 마치 예수님이 십자가를 지시듯이 유관순 열사 그 다 피지도 못한 소녀에게 이런 십자가를 주셨습니까 하고 부르짖습니다. 염통을 뚫고 나오는 애국의 절규 구구절절마다 비치는 핏자국이, 비치는 이 절규를 어찌 다듬고 고친다는 말입니까.

　이 시를 읽다가 쉬고 읽다가 다시 쉬곤 하면서 머리를 벽에 기대이고 나도 유관순 누나를 불러 봅니다. 그리고 흰 저고리 검은 치마를 입은 17세의 성녀의 모습을 떠올립니다. 형무소 의사가 적었다는 사인을 읽고 일본의 경찰이었든지 아니면 일본제국에 고용이 되었던 조선 경찰이었든지 알 수는 없지만 차마 인간으로서는 할 수 없는 만행에 몸이 떨립니다.

　생각하기 싫어 하는 지금의 세대에게 유관순 누님의 순교가 이 시를 써내려가는 시인의 절규가 얼마나 들릴지 모르지만 나라를 잃어 본 사람들만이 느낄 수 있는 이 통한의 일부라도 전할 수 있으면 하는 마음 간절합니다.

　가슴에서 터져 나오는 이 절규, 매 줄마다 어려있는 핏방울에 가칠을 할 용기도 수정을 할만한 기교도 없습니다.

　나도 시집을 읽으며 유관순 누님 어찌 그렇게 혼자 고통을 당하셨나요 하고 통곡을 하고 싶을 뿐입니다.

(임인년 늦은 겨울)

Whole Body is on Fire

　Reverend Paul Chang asked me to read his poems on Kwan Soon Yu. He sent them to me by e-mail.

　They touched my heart deeply. They took my breath away. I felt like I was actually listening to outcries of the patriot instead of reading poetry.

　Surely, these poems are heart-felt outcries, not poems of roses or peony blossoms. Every line of poems made me feel like I was witnessing blood of the patriot.

The patriot was born with predestined mission to be witness for the love of Korea. Her love of the country matured at Young-myung elementary school and Ewha school. The poet's calling for the martyred patriot whose life was sacrificed 97 years ago is nothing short of heart-wrenching laments.

The famous Korean poet So-wol wrote about his love in First Soul; "I call out your name··· The sound of my calling is missed... The gap between heaven and earth is too wide..." Like So-wol's longing heart for his love, the poet's calling for the patriot sounds like zigzagging lightnings among clouds. And the poet does not stop there. He goes on to say 'even if I stand here and turn into stone, I will call the same name, the name of my love'.

Then, he goes on to write poem #46. Continually, he runs to Young-myung school in Gongju, Ewha school, and Ahwoonae marketplace in Byeongchon city. As if he is entranced by a spirit, he runs calling the patriot's name, Kwan Soon Yu.

Then he kneels to God and pleads. He cries out to God 'how could you give such a young innocent girl a cross that Jesus had to bear?' They are poems of heart-wrenching and blood-stained cries.

I read poems, stopped, read some more, and stopped. Sometimes, I put my head on the wall and called the name, Kwan Soon Yu, in whisper. And I imagined a 17 years old saint dressed with white jeogori and black skirt. I shuddered at the atrocity committed by Japanese police, after reading the cause of her death.

I do not know whether the poems of patriotic martyr, Kwan Soon Yu, may appeal to our new generation that does not seem to like to think. I just hope they would understand even an iota of bitter grief that people who experienced loss of their own country know only.

Every sentence of poems is heart—wrenching and is coated with blood of patriotism. I dare not touch them to add or edit.

I just feel like crying and ask Kwan Soon Yu 'How could you suffer so much pain and so alone?'

2022

HyunBong, Yong Hae Lee

글을 마치며

유관순 열사와 더불어 긴 여행을 하고 돌아온 느낌이다.

영생을 믿는 목사로서 오래 전 구상하였던 글을 마칠 때까지 나와 대화해 주고 더욱이 열사가 가졌던 신앙심과 애국의 혼을 일깨워 준 많은 애국의 선열들의 응원에 진심으로 감사 드린다.

나라의 필연적 숙제인 통일과 국민대통합을 목전에 둔 저희들에게 열사는 그 길의 기초를 가르쳐 주었다.

"민족의 정체성(주체성)을 찾아라." 하늘나라에서 들려주는 소리요 부탁이다. 유관순 열사에 대한 시는 그의 얼을 이어받아 영구히 이어질 것을 믿고 바란다.

작은 시집이 나오기까지 여러 모로 후원해 주고 격려해 준 친구들과 동지들에게 감사를 드린다. 특히 서문을 써주신 최병현 시인, 독후감을 남겨준 이용해 작가 그리고 모든 시를 영문으로 번역해 주신 김리자, 고마운 분들이다. 이들의 이름을 이 시집과 더불어 영구히 남기고 싶다.

2022년 12월
장철우

On Finishing the Book

I feel as if I had a long trip with Kwan Soon Yu. As a pastor who believes in the eternal life, I am truly thankful to her for sharing dialogues with me until I finished the book. I am also thankful to her for awakening the spirit of love for my country. I am truly thankful to encouragement of many patriotic martyrs, too.

Unification is a huge challenge of our homeland. Patriot Kwan Soon Yu showed me the road to foundation of unification.

"Find the Identity of Korean People." That is the voice and request from Kingdom of God.

I hope these poems of patriot Kwan Soon Yu will serve as momentum for us to inherit her patriotic soul forever.

I would like to thank those who supported and encouraged me for making this publication possible. especially poet Byung Hyun Choi who wrote the introduction, Yong Hae Lee who

249

wrote comment after reading the book, and Lija Kim who was my English translator. I truly thank them for their support. I would like to leave their names in this book forever. I dedicate this book to patriot Kwan Soon Yu and deceased patriots of Korea with prayers.

영원히 불타오르는 별이 되어

1판 1쇄 발행 2022년 12월 25일
지은이   장철우
영 역   김리자
발행인   이선우
펴낸곳   도서출판 선우미디어
                Printed in Korea ⓒ 2022, 장철우
                1997. 8. 7 제305—2014—000020
                02643 서울시 동대문구 장한로 12길 40, 101동 203호
전화   2272—3351, 3352
팩스   2272—5540
전자주소   sunwoome@daum.net   greenessay2014@daum.net

정가   18,000원

※ 잘못된 책은 바꿔 드립니다.
※ 저자와 협의하여 인지 생략합니다.

ISBN 978—89—5658—724—0 03810

영원히 불 타오르는 별이 되어

영원히
불 타오르는
별이
되어

영원히 불 타오르는 별이 되어

영원히
불 타오르는
별이
되어

장철우 시 | 김리자 영역